As the horses paced along in rhythm, the sleigh bells made their distinctive sounds while the sleigh swished and glided across the snow. The outing was one of sheer enchantment, carrying her back to the other magical morning on the ski slopes with Raoul.

The scene right now was too surreal for Crystal. She closed her eyes for a little while and just listened as she dreamed about what it would be like if he had any deeper feelings for her.

Finally today, his kiss had brought her own feelings closer to the surface to be acknowledged. But Raoul wasn't her lover.

The kiss he'd given her in the bedroom was something he'd done in order to wake her up to the possibilities of life, but it hadn't been prompted by the earthshaking desire she had for him. When she'd told him she couldn't accept his offer to run a ski school here, he'd left it alone. His calm acceptance proved to her that he could compartmentalize his feelings for the good of the moment.

Dear Reader,

We've all heard the expression *true blue*. In terms of one's overall character, it means never wavering, solid, dependable for life!

In my novel, *Snowbound with Her Hero*, my heroine, Crystal, has learned to depend on her French brother-in-law, Raoul, who in time becomes her best friend. When destiny throws both of them a curve, they realize there's more to their deep abiding friendship and loyalty than either had suspected. Now this *true blue* hero is faced with the greatest dilemma of his life. A choice has to be made that will impact his life and Crystal's forever.

Hopefully you'll read this Christmas story to discover the choice he made.

Enjoy!

Rebecca Winters

REBECCA WINTERS
Snowbound with Her Hero

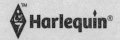

TORONTO NEW YORK LONDON
AMSTERDAM PARIS SYDNEY HAMBURG
STOCKHOLM ATHENS TOKYO MILAN MADRID
PRAGUE WARSAW BUDAPEST AUCKLAND

Recycling programs
for this product may
not exist in your area.

ISBN-13: 978-0-373-17763-9

SNOWBOUND WITH HER HERO

First North American Publication 2011

Printed in U.S.A.

Rebecca Winters, whose family of four children has now swelled to include three beautiful grandchildren, lives in Salt Lake City, Utah, in the land of the Rocky Mountains. With canyons and high Alpine meadows full of wildflowers, she never runs out of places to explore and they—along with her favorite vacation spots in Europe—often end up as backgrounds for her Harlequin Romance® novels. Writing is her passion, along with her family and church.

Rebecca loves to hear from her readers. If you wish to email her, please visit her website, www.cleanromances.com.

No one loves the Colorado Mountains more than my son John, who started out on skis early in life and now flies down the slopes of Breckenridge like a champion.
He's a wonderful son, husband and father, and the source of inspiration for this book. I've dedicated it to him.

CHAPTER ONE

"PHILIPPE? OVER HERE!" Crystal Broussard waved to her dark blond six-year-old son. She stood next to her father's car with the Marler Sports logo printed on the side. He came running out of the elementary-school entrance to the lineup of cars waiting. Being a Friday, the kids were out of school two hours earlier than usual.

Gusting winds had shifted from the southwest to the northwest, meaning a full-scale Colorado blizzard was on its way. Soon 10,000-foot Crystal Peak, her namesake, would be whited out along with the other surrounding peaks.

Crystal, who'd been put on skis as soon as she could walk, had been born in this 9,600-foot ski mecca and recognized the signs. The temperature had already dropped to the twenties. Soon the town of Breckenridge would be covered in even more snow, after several recent storms, the last one blanketing the area a few days ago.

It was good news for her father's business. Skiers from around the world flocked here and spent a lot of money on ski clothes and equipment. She'd worked part-time for her father while Philippe finished kindergarten; but now that he was a first-grader she was working full-time.

She gave him a huge hug, forcing him to reciprocate before opening the back door for him. "I've missed you today. Hurry and fasten yourself in. I want to drive us back to the store before the storm hits."

"Can't we just go home?"

That's all he ever wanted to do lately. Just go home and play quietly in his room…

"This won't take long. You need a new coat. This afternoon a shipment of parkas came in. There aren't too many in your size, so we need to get you in one you like before they're put out on the racks and taken." With Christmas in nine days, the last-minute rush for gifts would bring the shoppers in droves.

"I don't want a new coat."

"I know you don't, but you've grown and the sleeves are too short." Just now she'd almost said that the parka he was wearing had been bought in France, where they used to live, and he'd outgrown it. But she caught herself in time, afraid he'd go all quiet. She had a hunch he was hanging on to it because it was the one he'd brought with him when they'd left Chamonix.

Crystal needed to do something quick to help her son. Since school had started in the fall, he'd been less communicative. All she heard lately were troubled sighs coming out of him. He'd been a different child since his father's death fourteen months ago. Eric Broussard, one of France's great skiers, had taken a fatal fall during the downhill race in Cortina, Italy, and had died at the young age of twenty-eight, devastating everyone.

Two years earlier the Broussard family had already

been plagued by the death of Suzanne, the wife of their son, Raoul. The Broussards were an institution that owned and ran the 100-year-old premier alpine mountaineering guide club in the French Alps. The two brothers had been very close. Probably—and this was Crystal's private theory—it was because they'd never competed. Raoul lived for climbing and mountaineering. His wife, Suzanne, had shared his passion for the mountains. Eric only wanted to do one thing. Ski.

News of his passing sent the French ski world into mourning for a favorite son, but the hardest hit of all was to Crystal, who had to explain to a little five-year-old boy that his daddy wouldn't be coming home.

Crystal had been two years younger than Eric when she'd met and dated him. That was at a time when she'd been a member of the national women's ski team and had one bronze medal to her credit. After their marriage, they'd settled in Chamonix, France, where Eric had been born and raised on skis.

Two months after the funeral was over, Crystal had moved her and Philippe back to her parents' home in Breckenridge, hoping it would help both of them to recover and move on. To her chagrin, Philippe had slowly gone into a shell and nothing seemed to bring him out of it, not even her two younger, fun-loving sisters, Jenny and Laura. They were in their early twenties and came and went from the house between ski races.

When Crystal had brought them back to Colorado, Philippe had a tantrum the first time her father tried to take him skiing. Crystal realized it was too soon. Maybe Eric's death had put him off skiing forever. She hadn't tried to get him on skis again. He'd skied with her in Chamonix, but she didn't know if he'd really liked it or just did it because she did.

Lately she'd been doubting her own thoughts and feelings where he was concerned. Her boy was never enthusiastic about anything. At first she hadn't expected enthusiasm or excitement from him. But this depression seemed to be growing worse despite all the love her family gave him. According to his new teacher, he didn't even try to make friends with the kids in his first grade class.

The one time this fall she'd invited a boy for a play date after school, Philippe had been unwilling to share his toys or play at the nearby park. After the day had ended in disaster, she hadn't tried it again. The other boy's mother reciprocated, but Crystal knew it hadn't gone well because she hadn't called to make another play date.

It worried her he never wanted to talk about his father. He always brought up his uncle Raoul, the adored uncle who phoned once a month. But whatever they talked about, Philippe kept it to himself.

In the beginning he'd had conversations on the phone with his cousin Albert, but since school had started, things had changed. He didn't articulate his wishes or worries and closed up if she tried to get him to discuss his feelings. Not even the *grand-mère* and *grand-père* he loved had the power to bring a lasting smile to his face or eyes. They'd flown over two different times to visit, once bringing his loving aunt Vivige with them, but he still remained aloof.

Molly, the mother of three and one of the long-time employees at her father's store, had suggested earlier today that maybe he was upset having to share his mommy with her family. The comment had gotten Crystal thinking, deepening her guilt that she was failing her child somehow.

Here she'd believed that living with her parents and sisters would help Philippe feel secure and loved. She'd originally planned to get a condo close to their house. But a year later she was still staying in their family home because she'd hoped the closeness would help him to heal, but nothing seemed to be further from the truth.

What if Molly were right?

The thought devastated Crystal that he might be feeling shut out because of his perception that she paid too much attention to her own family. If she moved them to a nearby condo, maybe Philippe would like having her all to himself and he would start communicating more without anyone else around. Whatever it took, she was willing to try it because the next step was to seek professional help. They both needed it.

Tonight after she'd put Philippe to bed, she would discuss it with her parents and start looking for a new place. She would decorate it with the few furnishings from their condo in Chamonix that were still in storage. Philippe could help her.

Maybe seeing the things would make him open up. Naturally, when they'd first come back to Breckenridge, she'd tried to re-create Philippe's bedroom to make him feel at home, but if he saw everything else, maybe that's what he needed. It had to work. She was desperate!

Crystal drove into the town center of Breckenridge and parked around the back of the store. "Come on, honey." Grabbing his hand, she led them inside the rear entrance. They walked over to the load of new parkas hanging on the rack ready to be rolled out on to the floor.

She lifted two and held them in front of Philippe. "Which do you like better, the blue or the green?"

He studied them for a minute. "I guess that one." He touched the navy coat. It would be a nice match with his blue eyes, a shade darker than Eric's.

"All right. Let's see how it looks on you."

When he'd shed his other coat, she put it on him. "This looks terrific on you. Come on. Let's go find Grandpa and see what he thinks."

The store had at least a dozen customers keeping the staff busy. Molly was with a group of skiers, but she was the first to notice them come out of the back room. "Hey, Philippe. I like that parka on you. It fits you perfectly."

He muttered something indistinct and averted his eyes.

Crystal sent Molly a silent message that she was sorry for her son's lack of manners and looked around for her father. "Where's Dad?"

"He said he had an errand, but he'll be back."

She'd heard that before. When he got talking to one of his friends, it might be several hours. "I guess we'll go on home and show Nana. He'll be there later."

As they turned to walk into the back room, Crystal heard a male voice behind them say, *"Eh bien, mon gars. Tu me souviens?"*

The French spoken in a deep, familiar voice caused the blood to pound in Crystal's ears.

Raoul.

Philippe could never have forgotten him. As for Crystal…

Both of them swung around at the same time. *"Oncle Raoul!"* her son cried out in sheer happiness, echoing her unspoken response.

Philippe had said his name so loudly, every head in the store turned in his direction. He pulled his hand away from Crystal's and flew into the arms of Eric's thirty-two-year-old brother. Her son threw his arms around his neck, clutching him for dear life. The next thing she knew Raoul was rocking him. She didn't know which one of them was squeezing harder.

Over Philippe's shoulder Raoul shot her a glance from eyes she'd always thought of as midnight-blue. At the moment they were neither friendly nor hostile, yet she felt their deep penetration like she'd been injected with a near fatal dose of electricity.

"I was hoping to find out you hadn't left for the day." He spoke English in a cultured voice with less of a French accent than Eric had done. "The family told me you've been working for your father since you returned from Chamonix."

"Yes." She was so astonished to see him, she couldn't find the words.

"I'm surprised."

She took an extra breath, wondering what he'd meant by that remark, which could be taken several ways.

As if reading her mind he said, "I'd imagined that if nothing else, you would have gone into coaching some new upcoming sports star." He flashed one of his beautiful rare smiles. "There isn't a female champion who skis like Crystal Broussard. You have a style no one's been able to imitate."

"*Had,* you mean."

"No," he responded on a more sober note, not letting it go. "It will always be there because you honed it into an art form. The ski world lost a true star when you stopped competing. I, for one, am sorry that happened."

Crystal found it hard to swallow because his comment stunned her. With the problems in her marriage followed by Eric's death, that part of her life seemed to have taken a backseat. For Raoul to bring it up now wasn't only a surprise, it was…flattering, especially coming from him.

That was because he was such a revered athlete in his own right and always meant what he said. Little did he know the idea of becoming a coach had touched on one of her secret dreams. It shook her to realize he was the first person to recognize that need inside her.

In the past, while Suzanne had been alive, they'd often been on the same wavelength and she'd enjoyed that aspect of their relationship. Sometimes it had even upset her because she hadn't experienced it with Eric and didn't like feeling guilty about it.

"Thank you for the compliment, Raoul, but I've had my son to worry about."

"That's understandable, but it seems to me you could still do both. In fact I wondered why you didn't go back to competition after Philippe was born."

"You mean in Chamonix?"

"*Naturellement.*"

"I wanted to, but being a mother is a full-time job."

"For some women maybe, but you could have managed both." His dark eyes flashed. "You're too gifted."

Raoul really believed in her.

But when she'd talked to Eric about it, he'd clutched her under the chin. "You're the one who didn't mind us getting pregnant before we'd planned to," he'd said. "If we're both gone, who'll take care of the baby? I'm not keen on hiring a nanny."

Soon after Philippe was born, Eric hadn't been keen on much of anything but skiing. It eventually ruled his life. Without conscious thought she'd tried to be mother and father to their son.

All the while she was remembering the past, she'd been staring at Raoul. She couldn't help it. His black hair was longer than she remembered. It had a tendency to curl and looked slightly ruffled from the wind outside. He was an inch taller than Eric, who'd stood six feet two—the brothers were quite different in body build and coloring.

Eric had been born with the natural lean body of a skier. He and their sister, Vivige, a terrific skier in her own right, resembled their father in that regard and were dark blondes.

On the other hand Raoul, standing there in his black bomber jacket, possessed a more powerful build and had a darker olive complexion like their mother. Both men had the stamp of the good-looking Broussard family, and it had been bequeathed to her adorable Philippe, who clung to his uncle.

The sight of Raoul brought intense pleasure and pain in equal waves, plus too many other emotions Crystal didn't dare examine right now. She noticed the lines around his wide mouth had deepened since the last time she'd seen him. A year ago the whole Broussard family, including Philippe's three cousins, had driven to the airport in Geneva to see her and Philippe off to the States.

There was a haunted look about his Gallic features that was new. If she wasn't mistaken, she thought he'd lost a few pounds. The changes only made him more attractive, resurrecting more feelings of guilt for finding him so terribly appealing. That guilt had lain dormant while she'd been here in Colorado.

Where Eric had been dashing, Raoul was drop-dead gorgeous, a comment her friends on the ski team had pointed out many times. The Broussard brothers had a female following that extended throughout the sporting world.

"It's good to see you, Raoul," she finally managed to say, but she had to fight to keep her voice steady.

"Is it?" he challenged. She recognized the clipped, off-putting tone of voice he always seemed to use with her when he phoned to speak to Philippe.

Was that accusation she heard, or was she simply overreacting to the unexpected question? She couldn't describe how it had come across, but to her dismay it put her on the defensive. That was the last emotion she wanted him to be aware of.

"How can you even ask me that?" She forced a smile. "Of course it is, especially after such a long time. Philippe and I are just so surprised you're here, aren't we?"

Right before Christmas was one of the busiest times for the Broussards' business as Chamonix was a favorite winter wonderland. Crystal was surprised he could take the time off to come. She moved closer to give him a hug. Philippe was still in his arms, looking so ecstatic, she could hardly think.

Raoul's free arm enfolded her. "It's good to see you too, *ma belle,*" he whispered against her temple. He'd often called her that as a term of brotherly affection. "Life hasn't been the same without you around."

She could say the same about him. Being away from France, from him—she'd felt like she'd been in exile. It had been of her own making and Raoul was the reason.

Before he set Philippe down, he gave them both a brief kiss on the cheek. He smelled wonderful, evoking memories from a time that would never come again.

Philippe clung to Raoul's hand and threw his head back. Those blue eyes had stars in them, the first she'd seen in so long, she couldn't remember. "Come with us. I want to show you my nana's house!" The revelation that he'd missed his uncle this terribly hit her with blunt force.

"I'd like that if it's all right with your *maman.*"

Crystal drew in a quick breath. "We'd love you to come. Did you drive from Denver in a rental car?"

"Oui," he answered with a hint of irony.

Of course he had. She was a fool.

"Can I go to the house in his car, *Maman?*"

He'd been calling her Mommy for the last year. Now suddenly her bilingual son had reverted to French. Another revelation that gave her second sight. Philippe had been starved for the man he'd loved most in the world next to his own father. In truth he'd spent more time with Raoul over the years than he'd spent with Eric, who was always off training.

"S'il te plâit." Please, his eyes begged her. In that

moment he reminded her of Eric when he begged Crystal to forgive him for something he'd done, or *not* done after he'd promised. *All the unkept promises.* The memories assailed her, knocking her off balance.

"Yes, of course. But make sure you're strapped in."

Philippe jumped up and down with all the excitement that had been missing since before Eric's death. The sight of his uncle had made a remarkable change in him.

"I'll take care of him," Raoul assured her in an aside.

He hadn't needed to say anything. Ever since the night she'd gone into labor two weeks early and Raoul had driven her to the hospital, comforting her on the way because she was bleeding, a bond had formed. She knew she could trust him with her life. He and Suzanne couldn't do enough to be there for her.

Eric had been away at a World Cup race in Cortina. It wasn't his fault he'd missed the delivery. The doctor hadn't expected her to have the baby so soon. When she'd called her mother-in-law for help, Raoul happened to be at the house and answered the phone. The second he heard the alarm in her voice, he'd dropped everything to help her. The doctor said his quick response had saved her life. Another ten minutes and she would have bled to death.

Watching Philippe cling to his uncle's arm brought back a rush of memories. "We'll follow you, Mommy!"

"Sounds good. I'll pull around the front." She turned away and hurried into the back room for Philippe's other parka, but her legs were wobbly because she was in shock. By the time she'd climbed in the car and started the motor, fear had snaked through her nervous system.

There was only one reason Raoul would have flown to the States. He'd brought bad news that he felt should be delivered in person. *He shouldn't have come.* A phone call would have been better.

She could speculate all she wanted, but whatever was wrong she didn't think she could handle the pain. They'd all lived through so much with two deaths in the family on top of her trying to bring Philippe out of his depression and help him cope. Yet Raoul was here now, and whatever emergency had brought him here, she would have to deal with it and be strong for Philippe no matter what.

The first fat snowflakes slapped against the windshield, harbingers of what was coming. Through the rearview mirror she watched the white Ford rental car trail behind her. Her heart refused to behave. It really was Raoul behind the wheel. He was in Breckenridge, not Chamonix.

Normally if he left town for any length of time, it was to climb or hike another range of mountains with his best friend, Des, whose home was in the Spanish Pyrenees. When they'd met Des on different occasions, she'd liked him very much. After Suzanne's death, the two men had spent over two months climbing in the Himalayas. Des had worried about Raoul.

So had she. For a long time after that, Raoul had been so closed up it was like his heart had gone into a deep freeze. Only around Philippe or Vivige's children had she seen it melt and remind her of the warm, wonderful man he'd once been when Suzanne was alive.

Crystal shivered, remembering that time when the

whole family had been so concerned about him. On a personal level, she'd lost a dear friend in Suzanne. Eric had thought the world of her, too. Until her death, when Raoul's world had collapsed, the four of them had done a lot together.

She bit her lip. A year had gone by without seeing him, except to hear his voice when he called and they spoke briefly before he asked to speak to Philippe. She heard snippets about him in conjunction with the family business, but she knew little about his personal life except for one thing.

The last time she'd talked to Vivige, she'd learned Raoul was seeing some woman named Sylvie Beliveau. The family was hoping it would grow into something serious and were keeping their fingers crossed.

Crystal had tried not to let the news affect her and refused to pry. Aside from her worry over Philippe, she wouldn't allow any painful reminders from the past to disturb this time of putting a new life together.

It sounded like Raoul had finally come out of his own darkness and was trying to get on with his life. She wished she didn't want to know what the other woman was like, but certain thoughts pervaded her mind anyway. And now Raoul was here.

Because of his unanticipated arrival this afternoon, her emotions were in chaos and the last year apart might never have been. Already a new form of turmoil was eating away at her insides, destroying whatever little peace of mind she'd been clinging to because an ocean had separated them.

Raoul had fastened Philippe in the backseat, but kept looking at him through the rearview mirror. Philippe could see him in it and they both smiled. "You've grown a foot since the last time I saw you." He spoke in French.

His nephew giggled. "I've had a birthday, too," he responded in the same language. "The model car you sent me is my favorite toy."

"I'm glad you like it."

"Next year I'll be seven."

Puzzled by the comment Raoul said, "How come you're in such a hurry to get older?"

"'Cause then Mommy will take me back to see you."

Stunned by the revealing comment, he had to take a fortifying breath. "Do you know how much I've missed you?" Raoul couldn't imagine loving his own child more than he loved Philippe.

The boy nodded. "I've missed you, too. Every time we talked on the phone, you promised you'd come and see me. How come it took you so long?"

He gripped the steering wheel tighter. There were several reasons. He hadn't liked the fact that he'd developed an unwanted attraction to his sister-in-law. It was better they were apart. For a long time he'd been at war with himself to keep things that way. But Philippe didn't know that, and there was only one safe answer to give him.

"Business has kept me too busy. Your grandfather has been forced to slow down, so I've been doing some of his work along with my own."

"Now that you're here you can stay at my nana's with me in the other bed. Sometimes Mommy sleeps in there with me when I cry."

Raoul sucked in his breath. "Do you cry a lot?"

"Yes. Do you?"

"Sometimes. I miss your father, too."

"I wish he didn't have to die. Then we wouldn't have to live here."

The tremor in his nephew's voice caused Raoul's throat to swell. "I've wished that a thousand times, Philippe." *A thousand times.* Crystal's decision to move back to Colorado had angered him. But as the months had worn on and he'd recovered from his initial reaction, he'd realized it was because he'd missed her.

They'd shared a hell of a lot over the years. When she'd left Chamonix for good, he was flung into another void that had nothing to do with the loss of his brother. Insane as it was, he found his thoughts dwelling on her all the time, filling him with guilt that it was *she* rather than Eric he was missing.

"I'm mad at Mommy."

Join the club, Philippe.

But Raoul steeled himself not to react. There'd been a major change in Crystal even before Eric's death. Emotionally he'd felt her push herself away from the family, from him. For his own sense of self-preservation he'd honored the unspoken message to stay away until now. On the flight over, part of him was still fighting the imminent reunion while the other part of him couldn't wait for it.

He'd stepped off the plane totally conflicted, but seeing her this afternoon brought a whole new set of feelings into the mix.

She no longer had that vivacious girl-next-door look that had been so appealing, she'd made the cover of every sporting magazine and had snared his brother. Their romance had captured the headlines for a long time. For him to have died so young, and leaving a wife and child behind, had taken its toll on everyone.

Remembering Philippe he said, "Why are you upset with your mother?"

"She made us come here. I want to go home."

There was an unmistakable forlornness in his tone. "Doesn't Breckenridge feel like home now?"

"No," came the quiet answer. "My house is in Chamonix."

So it was... For a six-year-old, Philippe had an intelligence and maturity beyond his years.

"Could I go home with you, Uncle Raoul?"

With that question, Raoul's thoughts reeled. Since there were things he couldn't discuss with his nephew until after he'd talked with Crystal, he pretended to misunderstand. "I've got a room at the Hotel Des Alpes down the road from your grandpa's store. If your mother says it's all right, you can sleep with me tonight."

"Goody! I always wanted to stay there. It has real sleigh bells inside. Sometimes Mommy lets me go inside to shake them."

He smiled because everything about Philippe was so endearing. "You like sleigh bells?"

"Yup. They're like the ones in Grandpa's storeroom. Remember when you took me and Albert for a sleigh ride?"

It surprised him Philippe remembered so much. Twelve months had passed since they'd left France, yet that memory had stood out. Was Crystal aware of her son's deepest feelings? Or was she still in too much pain over losing Eric to feel anything these days?

Raoul had gone through the grieving period after

Suzanne was killed, but he'd got past it. If they'd had a child together already, it might have taken longer if you saw the face of the person you'd loved every time you looked at your own child. But that hadn't been the case.

"Tell me about school. What's your teacher's name?"

"Ms. Crabtree."

"Do you like your teacher?"

"She's all right, but she can't speak French. Nobody speaks French here."

He spoke in a voice that said he was bored with the idiocy of people, reminding Raoul of Eric when his brother brushed aside something he found irritating during a conversation. Raoul didn't know whether to laugh or cry. Being with Philippe made the memories fly fast and furiously.

"Your mommy speaks French." When there was no comment he said, "Have you got a best friend yet?"

"Nope. Albert's my best friend." Albert was Philippe's seven-year-old cousin.

"How come you haven't made one here?"

"I just haven't." A sigh escaped.

That was no answer. There was a lot wrong with Philippe. "You have *me*."

"But you live in Chamonix and Mommy won't take me home." His nephew's tears weren't far away.

"Have you asked her?"

"Yes. But she always cries when I do. My nana told me Mommy's going to take me back when I'm older, but I want to go now. I wish I could live with you."

Raoul's eyes smarted. When he'd driven up here from Denver, he'd imagined he'd find an Americanized boy who'd forgotten his French and Raoul. He had to clear his throat. "Then your mother would feel bad."

"I don't care."

"That's not true," he said gently.

"She's mean."

"I don't believe it."

"But she is. When I ask her if I can call you up, she says we have to wait till you call first because you're too busy."

Raoul bit down hard. "I'll have a talk with her about that." It was his fault. By trying to distance himself from Crystal, he'd gone too far. But that was because of his unbrotherly feelings for her that he'd been trying to fight—without success.

"She'll get mad I told you."

"Does she really get mad?"

After a pause Philippe said, "No, but she doesn't smile."

Once long ago Crystal's beautiful smile had been her trademark. "We like our mothers to smile, don't we?" No matter how much pain everyone is in.

Through the mirror he saw Philippe nod.

When Raoul had watched her jet take off for Colorado, he'd felt like a dark shield had dropped over him. He hadn't been able to imagine himself smiling again. "Who do you play with at school?"

"Nobody."

His heart lurched. "Tell me the truth now."

Philippe's little chin jutted out. "I am."

"What do you think is the problem?"

"I heard a couple of the boys talking at recess. They said I'm a geek and have a stupid name."

Just now Philippe sounded like the brother who'd

grown up with Raoul. When Eric got upset, he became obstinate and defensive. It took a lot to pull him out of it. "I bet your teacher is impressed you speak two languages. Those boys are just jealous."

"What does 'jealous' mean?"

"They wish they could be as smart as you. But since they only speak English, they're mad and say mean things."

"Oh."

By the time they reached the mountain home made of wood and glass, Raoul realized his nephew had been living in pain. Unfortunately, the news Raoul had brought meant there was more ahead.

He stepped out of the car into a serious snowstorm and opened the back door for Philippe. "Come on. Let's get you in the house." He picked up his nephew and gave him another hug before carrying him up the front steps. On the way he saw Christmas lights twinkling in the window.

Crystal had opened the door for them. The scent of pine wafted past him. Her mother, Liz, flew across the foyer to greet him with a strong hug. On dozens of occasions when Crystal's parents had come to Chamonix, he'd had the opportunity to spend time with the charming blond woman.

She invited him into the den, which was lined with family pictures, many of them showing Crystal winning ski races with her face rosy and glowing. Several showed her and Eric together, their arms around each other.

This was the first time Raoul had been to Breckenridge, let alone to Crystal's family home. Though Chamonix and Breckenridge were an ocean apart, being here made him realize how similar their two families' upbringings had been.

The room had been decked out for Christmas. Their tree with its many colored lights stood in front of the picture window just like the one at his parents' home, except the decorations were different.

A few days ago he and his brother-in-law, Bernard, who ran an engineering firm for a petroleum business in Chamonix, had set up a Christmas tree for Raoul's mother in the salon. They'd strung it with the traditional white lights. Vivige had organized their children to put on the ornaments. When Christmas Eve came, the wax candles in the tree's candle holders would be lighted after they returned from Mass.

That is, if there was going to be a Christmas Eve this year not marred by more tragedy.

He removed his coat. "You have a beautiful home, Liz," he said at last, gravitating to the warmth coming from the grate fire.

"Thank you. Please sit down and make yourself comfortable."

After peeling off Philippe's new coat, she asked her daughter to bring in the appetizers and drinks from the kitchen. "When Crystal called and told me you were on your way up to the house with Philippe, I phoned Todd. He's thrilled you've come and he's going to bring home pizza for us."

"Goody! That's my favorite." Philippe's eyes lit on Raoul. "Do you want to see my new computer game? It's upstairs in my room."

"*Bien sûr.*" He glanced at Crystal to get her permission. In the firelight her iridescent blue eyes looked haunted. "Is that all right?"

"Of course." She'd shed her parka and sat on the end of the couch in jeans and a cherry-colored crewneck sweater. The mold of her curves was the same, but since the last time he'd seen her taking some painkiller while she was waiting for their flight to be called, she'd had her hair cut. Instead of trailing down her back, her hair swished against her shoulders from a side part.

There were other differences, too. As he got up from the chair to join Philippe, it dawned on him the high color he'd always associated with her complexion was missing. Once she'd become pregnant, she'd given up competition skiing. But looking at her right now, she couldn't even have been doing much pleasure skiing these days. He wished to heaven he didn't care.

CHAPTER TWO

AFTER DINNER, Philippe begged Raoul to go back upstairs again. Crystal remained behind in the den and
talked with her parents in order to give her son private
time with his uncle. No one was deceived that he'd
come for any other reason than to bring news she didn't
want to hear. But she recognized that Raoul hadn't let
on anything so as not to alarm Philippe.

"Are you all right, honey?" her dad asked.

"Not really." But it wasn't something she could discuss with anyone. Once Philippe had actually eaten a
whole piece of pizza, they'd disappeared and had been
conspicuous by their absence. She checked her watch.

"It's past Philippe's bedtime." She excused herself,
gave her father a kiss and walked upstairs with pounding heart. On the way down the hall she heard her son
whooping it up. The happy sounds were followed by
his uncle's deep laughter. Philippe had been morose
for so long, it was a shock to hear and see him this ani-
mated.

When she entered his bedroom, she found him and
Raoul having a game of checkers on his bed. His face
was flushed with excitement because he was winning.

"I hate to break this up, but it's time for bed, honey."

To her surprise he scrambled right off the covers without having to be coaxed. "Uncle Raoul's going to let me stay with him tonight."

That was news to Crystal. She shook her head. "There's a blizzard outside. I don't want you going out in it."

Raoul stayed on the bed without saying anything. She could feel his unsettling gaze focused on her.

Philippe pointed to the other bed. "Then he can sleep with me."

Her son had it all worked out. If he didn't get his way tonight, there was going to be a war, which in the end she wouldn't win. Heaving a sigh she said, "Tell you what. Grab yourself some pajamas and take your bath. While you do that, I'll talk to your uncle. Okay?"

"Okay. Don't go anywhere, Uncle Raoul."

"I'll stay right here."

"See you in a minute."

Philippe pulled his green pajamas with dinosaurs from the dresser. On top of it sat Eric's last framed gold medal won in the men's downhill. Her bronze medal, won for the women's downhill, had been framed and was propped next to it. All his other medals were back in Chamonix at his parents' home. Crystal wanted it that way. The Broussards were so proud of their son. One day when Philippe was grown and had his own place for them, he would want them for himself.

The minute he'd dashed down the hall to the bathroom, she sank down on the other twin bed with her hands on either side to brace herself for whatever was coming. "This is the first chance we've had to talk alone. My parents and I are aware you're here because of some kind of emergency." She couldn't prevent the tremor in her voice. "Tell me now before Philippe comes bursting back in the room."

Raoul put the checkers in the box and got to his feet. His hard muscled physique dominated the room. "Papa came down with a cold two weeks ago that turned into the flu. It hung on and now he has pneumonia. He's been hospitalized because his asthma flared up again after all these years and has complicated his condition. The doctor says if he doesn't rally pretty soon, we could lose him by Christmas."

Crystal's cry resounded in the bedroom. "He can't die, Raoul. He just can't!" She jumped to her feet, hugging her arms to her waist. That was only nine days away. She loved her father-in-law—in fact, the whole family. So did Philippe.

"Mother believes it would do his spirits good if he were to see his grandson again. I agree it would be the best medicine and told her I'd come and talk to you about it in person."

She averted her eyes, but couldn't prevent the groan that escaped her throat.

"I'm not unaware you're building a life for yourself here, Crystal. To fly back to France with Philippe would open up the wound again, but, for all our sakes, I'm asking you to do this. After we buried Eric, Papa worked harder than ever to stave off his grief, but now that he's ill, he has too much time to think and remember."

Crystal could relate. All she'd done was think and remember. Jules—Raoul's father—was still mourning Suzanne's death, too. All of them had loved her. Two deaths in one family were simply too much. No one understood that better than Crystal.

"I'm so sorry about Jules. This has to be agonizing for everyone." Especially this soon after Eric. When Raoul didn't say anything, she eyed him again. "I'm afraid this is hardest on you. With your father in the hospital, you have the whole weight of the family business on your shoulders."

"Sometimes more work is a blessing." He darted her a probing glance "Haven't you found that's true, too?"

"Yes," she murmured before looking away guiltily. While Philippe was at school, she'd put in all kinds of extra hours dealing with stock in the back room of her father's store so she wouldn't think. If she hadn't let Eric's indifference cause her to lose her own identity as a skiing champion, she could be in an entirely different place right now.

Raoul's unexpected arrival had exposed her deepest concerns and feelings on that score. He made her realize she needed to do something about herself, but for the immediate moment her thoughts were focused on Jules and what would help him most to recover.

"Are your passports still current? Otherwise I'll request an emergency visa." He took her capitulation as *a fait accompli*.

This was one time she had to give in and go. She wanted to, despite all her fears. "That won't be necessary. Ours are good for another two years."

"*Bon.* Then we'll fly back tomorrow."

Her thoughts reeled. It meant being with him again, talking to him during the long flight. Obviously the adage of out of sight, out of mind hadn't worked in her case. She was too thrilled to see him again and had to admit it.

"I took the liberty of making a reservation for the two of you in case you were willing to come." Raoul was a brilliant man who never left anything to chance. "I wouldn't worry about Philippe missing school," he said when she didn't respond. "After what he told me on the way here in the car, I think a trip home to Chamonix is the medicine he needs, too."

Home to Chamonix. Those words shook her to the depths. Her breath caught.

"Wh-what did he tell you?" she stammered.

A grimace marred Raoul's features. "What *didn't* he tell me? But he's out in the hall now, which doesn't give me time to go over the list."

No sooner had he spoken than Philippe came bouncing back in the room. Raoul's hearing had to be more acute than hers because she hadn't heard anything except the loud thud of her own heart.

Philippe stared at both of them. "Can he stay with us tonight?"

The pleading look in those blue eyes combined with the palpable tension coming from Raoul was too much to take. It hurt her that Philippe had felt comfortable enough to tell Raoul things she hadn't been able to get out of him. But that was the possessive mother in her talking, and this situation with Philippe was about him, not her.

She moistened her lips nervously, aware of Raoul's piercing glance. "I have a better idea, honey. Your uncle's things are back at the hotel. After flying all this way, he needs a good sleep in a big bed." Before her son had time for a fresh meltdown she added, "And *we* need time to get *our* things packed."

The tears filling his eyes stopped short of dripping down his cheeks. "Where are we going?"

Crystal smoothed her hands over her hips in an unconscious gesture. "I'll let your uncle tell you." Above all else, she trusted his discretion.

Raoul got down on his haunches in front of Philippe. "Your *grand-père* isn't feeling very well right now, and he's missing his *petit-fils.* So I told him I would fly to Colorado and bring you and your mommy back with me. When he sees you, I have an idea he'll get better in a big hurry. How does that sound?"

She knew how it sounded to Philippe. The only sounds in the room came from his happy sobs as he launched himself into Raoul's arms. They were such deep sobs, it pained her to think of the damage she'd unwittingly done by staying away from Chamonix so long.

Needing to channel her energy, she went to the closet and pulled down the suitcase she'd stored on one of the shelves. Her eye caught sight of his little striped robe hanging on a hanger. He'd outgrown it, too, but she hadn't thrown away any of the clothes they'd brought with them. She couldn't. Suddenly her emotions erupted and she buried her face in the toweling.

"Crystal?"

She quickly wiped off the moisture before turning around. Raoul stood in the doorway to the closet. There wasn't enough distance separating them for her to breathe normally. His eyes studied her, but she couldn't read their expression. "I sent Philippe downstairs to tell your parents."

Another necessary distraction for her son. Raoul

had a way with Philippe. While she stood there try-ing to gather her wits, he picked up the suitcase and moved it to one of the beds. She followed, watching as his fingers smoothed the Chamonix sticker pasted on the outside lid.

It brought back a memory of Raoul buying the sticker at the airport. He'd put it on Philippe's suit-case. "This is so you won't forget me." He'd kissed his nephew, who'd been in tears. His finger motion just now conveyed the feelings of that painful day more powerfully than any words could do. It sent a tremor through her body. She'd never forgotten Raoul. That would be impossible.

"What time is check-in at the airport in the morn-ing?"

Her question seemed to jar him from his thoughts. He lifted his dark head. "Eight o'clock."

"With this storm, we'll have to leave Breckenridge by five to make it."

Through his dark lashes he flashed her a shuttered glance. "I'll be here. We can eat breakfast at the air-port while we're waiting to board our flight."

She nodded and opened the suitcase. "We'll be ready."

Philippe came running back in the room. "Nana and Grandpa said they're going to miss me, but I told them *Grand-père* is sick and missed me, too." He looked up at Raoul with a soulful expression. "Do you have to leave now?"

"Don't worry." He swept Philippe up in his arms once more. "We'll see each other first thing in the morning. Right now you need to mind your mother and go to sleep because it'll be a long flight to Geneva tomorrow."

"That's not Chamonix."

Raoul chuckled. "No. Geneva's in Switzerland. We'll pick up my car at the airport and drive home."

"Will it take a long time?"

"Only about an hour."

Philippe looked at Crystal. "Will we go to *our* house?"

The house he was referring to had actually been a condo she and Eric had rented. At one time she'd assumed they would buy a house of their own, but as problems arose in their marriage no one knew about and still didn't, they'd kept putting it off.

"Someone else lives there now," she replied quietly. He needed to know the truth up front so there'd be one less expectation when they got there.

"That's okay. We'll stay with Uncle Raoul."

"No, Philippe—" Crystal blurted. *No*... "H-he has a girlfriend," she said, her voice faltering.

"You do?"

Something flickered in the depths of Raoul's eyes. "But she doesn't live with me, *mon gars,* and there's nothing I'd love more than to have you sleep at my house," he inserted in a smooth tone without looking at her.

"We'll be staying at your grandparents', honey."

"That's right. Your *grand-mère* has your dad's old room all ready for you and your mother. She can't wait to spoil you. Come on and walk me downstairs."

Philippe grabbed his hand and the two of them headed out of the room. The fact that Raoul didn't deny the existence of a girlfriend verified Vivige's information. It should have come as a relief. But as Crystal followed them, she felt a whole new nightmare beginning.

Geneva was one of Europe's main hubs. After disembarking, they wove their way through the crowds to the parking area. Crystal watched Raoul stow the last of their bags in the trunk of his car before getting behind the wheel. Philippe had already climbed in the back and strapped himself in. The sleek black vehicle was a recent acquisition, but Raoul had never been a sports car fan like his brother. As far as she was concerned, this sedan was the ultimate in comfort and luxury.

Within a few minutes they'd wound their way out of the airport. She checked her watch. Barring unforeseen circumstances they'd be in Chamonix by noon. The long fifteen-hour flight was finally over.

Philippe had been restless for part of it, but between her and Raoul, they'd kept him occupied while they took turns napping. Philippe ought to have been exhausted by now, but he showed no signs of it yet.

She turned her head around. "Are you hungry, honey?"

"Yes. Can we get some chicken nuggets?"

"I'm afraid they don't have them here."

"Actually they do," Raoul informed them, darting her an amused glance. "There've been a few changes while you've been away."

She lifted her brows. "Even the Swiss caved for fast food. That's really saying something."

Her response brought a smile to his lips that melted her insides. "I'm glad they did. I come down here often enough to meet with the heads of groups who want to arrange a special climb and I'm usually in a hurry. It saves time to be able to pick up a snack en route without getting out of the car."

Before long they'd all eaten and were on their way again. During the drive Raoul phoned his mother to let her know they would be there shortly. From what Crystal could gather, his father was no better, but no worse, thank heaven.

After he hung up he spoke sotto voce. "I'll take you to the house first so you can freshen up."

The "house" hardly described the Broussard family home. It was a marvelous old brown-and-white three-story chalet located in Les Pecles, a few minutes from the town center of Chamonix. The first Broussard, a famous alpinist, built it 220 years earlier in the *haut-savoyard* style. The mountaineering tradition had carried down through the years, making their name a household word for Alpine adventure throughout the French Alps.

Due to its location on the Swiss and Italian border, there was an international flavor that made the town cosmopolitan and brought visitors from all over the world. No matter the season, Crystal thought it the most beautiful place on earth. Seeing it again with all the streets and shops decked out for Christmas brought memories, both good and bad. Hearing the ecstatic sounds coming from Philippe she knew he was in heaven to be back.

"I see the peak!" he called out excitedly.

They'd approached the snow-covered Chamonix valley from the north, dominated by Mont Blanc, but he was referring to the Aiguille du Midi. Raoul had taken her and Philippe up on it in the cable car. After that experience it had been *the* landmark for her son among a world of mountains and peaks on both sides of the town of 15,000 sprawled through the valley.

"Do you remember what it's called, honey?"

"No, but Uncle Raoul said the sun sits on it. See?"

Out of the corner of her eye she saw Raoul smile. "You have a good memory, Philippe."

Crystal turned her head abruptly to look out the passenger window. Once Philippe had been born, many of her memories had to do with Raoul being with them rather than Eric. After Suzanne died, Crystal and Philippe had spent a lot of time with him and his family while they all mourned.

Eric gave his love and support when he could, but he had to train through all the seasons and was gone a great deal. Crystal felt he was away too much and reminded him they had a son who was missing him terribly.

A year before he'd died, she'd begged for them to live part of the year in Breckenridge, where they could both train and he'd find more time to be with their son away from his family. There hadn't been too much togetherness. She didn't tell him Philippe went to Raoul for everything. That would only upset him, but the situation couldn't go on.

To her chagrin Eric didn't like the idea of actually living away for even part of a year. He'd told her they would buy a house. In other words, he hoped a new project would keep her busy. It didn't occur to him she might like to start up racing again.

She told him a house wouldn't be a substitute for a full-time father. Over the months that followed, she realized he was too entrenched with his lifestyle and friends, too comfortable with the way things were, to want to leave. They didn't have a marriage anymore.

Eric had been surrounded by a loving support group from the time he was born. Crystal had joined it by becoming his wife, but there was one little body who had needed his attention more of the time now. A day or two here and there between races that took him to other parts of Europe and the States for longer periods wasn't enough for Philippe.

The more she'd brought it up to her husband, the more irritated he became until they had nothing between them. Having been a top athlete herself, he thought she understood the demands on him. She *did* understand, at the time. But priorities changed once a child came into the world.

The day he'd left for Cortina, she'd reminded him of that fact and told him she was going back to Breckenridge with Philippe to stay for a few months until he realized what he was missing and come for them.

He'd remained mute. After giving Philippe a hug and a kiss, he'd walked past her and slammed the door on his way out of their condo. He'd never done that before. That was the last time she'd seen him alive.

"There's *Grand-mère!*"

Philippe's cry brought Crystal out of her torturous thoughts. The second Raoul stopped the car, her son opened the rear door and ran up the few steps into her arms. They hugged for a long time.

Crystal's sixty-three-year-old mother-in-law, Arlette, was lean and athletic like her children, possessing endless energy. She and Jules were very alike, always busy, always cordial and always welcoming company into their home.

From a distance, everything about her appeared to look the same. That was until Crystal got out before Raoul could help her and hurried toward his mother, noticing new worry lines on her attractive features. Since the last time she'd seen her, there was a touch more gray in the dark hair she wore short. It gave her an added sophistication.

Arlette clapped her hands on Crystal's cheeks. "*Mon Dieu,* you've come and brought Philippe. Jules will be overjoyed. We've missed you both so much."

Crystal hugged her hard, thinking Arlette was a little thinner. Because she was shorter than Crystal's five-foot-seven frame, she seemed even smaller to her this time. "We've missed you, too," she whispered. "I can't bear it that Jules is so ill."

"Neither can I." The older woman wiped her eyes. "Now that you've come, I know he'll start to feel better."

"I pray that's true." As she looked around, she realized Philippe had gone inside the house with Raoul. Arlette hooked her arm through Crystal's and drew her past the door. Once it was closed, they went up the stairs to the first floor. The place had been transformed into a Christmas fairyland.

"It's beautiful, Arlette."

"We can thank Raoul. He got Bernard to help him set up everything for me."

What would their family do without Raoul? He carried the emotional weight and still managed to do his own work and everyone else's. Crystal marveled at his capacity.

Philippe ran over to the tree. "There's *Père Noël!*" *He remembered.*

"Don't touch it, honey. Those wooden ornaments are very precious."

"He can touch whatever he wants," Arlette countered, like the loving grandmother she was. "Go ahead, Philippe. Take it off the branch. It's yours to keep."

"Goody!"

"You can have a piece of marzipan in that candy dish, too."

"Mmm." He stuffed one in his mouth while he ran over to inspect the fabulous hand-painted grandfather clock that had just struck the half hour. Philippe had always loved to stand in front of it and wait to hear the chimes. Little Hansel and Gretel figures came out, fascinating him.

"I've put your suitcases in the upstairs bedroom," Raoul informed Crystal. He'd just walked into the room still wearing his bomber jacket. She took one look at him and felt her heart turn over and over. It had been doing that since the moment she'd heard his voice at her father's store, almost as if it had a life of its own.

"Thank you."

"Hey—here's my daddy!" Philippe cried out with his mouth still full of candy. With the small, red-painted wooden figure of a solemn Father Christmas clutched in one hand, her son used his other hand to pick up a small framed picture of his father in his ski outfit. Arlette had placed it on the long credenza with many other family pictures. Everyone in the family was represented.

He picked up another picture and showed it to Raoul. "This is *Tante* Suzanne, huh?"

Crystal squeezed her eyes closed for a second. This was the hard part.

"Yes."

"She died, huh."

"That's right."

"Was she skiing like Daddy?"

"No. It was spring and she died in an aerial tram accident."

Suzanne had gone hiking with some people from the office where she'd worked. They'd taken an aerial tram so they could start their hike way up in the mountains. But it had been hit by gale force winds and fell, killing her. Crystal winced to think about the bare bones details again.

"Oh," Philippe said in a quiet voice. "Do you still cry?"

"Not anymore, but I'll never forget her."

Philippe let out a big sigh and wandered over to his uncle, putting an arm around him. "I don't cry as much, either." *Oh, Philippe.* "Mommy says Daddy's in heaven. Do you think Suzanne's in heaven, too?"

"Yes."

The scene was too much for Arlette, whose eyes had filled. With a husband lying ill, she didn't need more of this conversation.

"Come on, honey." Crystal took hold of his hand. "We need to go upstairs and freshen up. Then we'll go over to the hospital to see your grandfather."

Philippe pulled back and looked up at her in alarm. "How come he's in there?"

"Remember your uncle told you he was sick?"

"Yes," he said in a tentative voice.

"Well, the hospital is the best place for him to get better."

"Does he know I'm coming?" he asked as Crystal walked up the stairs to the next floor with him.

"I don't think so. It's supposed to be a surprise."

"I like surprises."

"He will too when he sees you walk in his room."

Crystal didn't need to ask where Arlette had put them. Raoul had already told them. Since Philippe's birth, Eric's old room had a double and a twin bed. On the dresser someone had put up a little Christmas tree with lights. More of Raoul's doing? Along with the décor there were some games and dozens of his father's mementos and trophies for Philippe to enjoy.

Photos of Eric at different ages lined one wall. Another one held pictures of baby Philippe's christening at St. Michel church, plus more pictures of the three of them. Eric and his son looked almost identical at the age Philippe was now. Her boy was delighted by everything.

She thought she might not be able to handle this painful trip down memory lane, but it turned out she was wrong. If anything, she looked at the smiling couple and their baby with the perspective of time on her side.

The birth of Philippe and the few weeks after when Eric had spent more time at home to be with her and the baby had been the last period of happiness in their marriage. Once the weighty responsibility of parenthood had descended, she'd thrown herself into it with the kind of joy she couldn't have imagined before becoming a mother. But in so doing, she'd caused an unwitting division between her and Eric that had only grown wider and unbridgeable with time.

Today she could admit the truth to herself. If he hadn't died, she knew deep inside she would have ended up in Breckenridge and a divorce would have followed. What was the old adage? Dignity in death, disgrace in divorce? It was an awful saying. In both cases there was loss. Period.

Raoul went inside the hospital room ahead of the others. He saw a new addition to all the flowers since he'd last been in here. A beautiful Christmas red poinsettia had been delivered. The get-well card was from Crystal's parents. Jules would be touched.

His thoughts flew to Philippe. He knew it would frighten him to see his graying grandfather on oxygen with an IV in his arm. In the last few weeks he'd lost ten pounds with the flu. His gaunt appearance made him look closer to seventy than sixty-five.

The doctor couldn't account for Jules getting so ill at his age, but they both agreed the two deaths in the family had probably been too much for him. Despite all his hard work, he was a family man through and through and lived for his children. Eric's death had robbed him of his joie de vivre. If anyone could bring it back, it would be Philippe, who had certain mannerisms and features inherited from his father.

"Papa?"

"Ah, Raoul. You've been gone so long." He grasped his hand and wept.

It killed him to see his father like this. "I've brought someone with me. Are you up for company?"

His eyelids fluttered open to half mast. *"Bien sûr,"* he murmured in a voice half as strong as normal.

"I'll be right back."

He hurried over to the door and opened it. Three worried pairs of eyes fastened on him. "How is he?" his mother asked.

"He's awake."

"Can I see him?" Philippe whispered.

"What do you think?" He reached for his nephew's hand and they walked over to the left side of the bed. Crystal and his mother followed and stood on the right. Raoul was surprised Philippe didn't flinch at all the tubes.

"Hi, *Grand-père.* It's me."

Again his father's eyelids opened, alert to a new voice in the room. "Me, who?"

Philippe giggled. "You know who I am." In case Jules couldn't see him well, Raoul lifted him in his arms.

His father's gray-blue eyes swerved to his grandson before glazing over with tears. "Ah...my boy, my boy. Come closer and give your *grand-père* a kiss." Raoul lowered him. "Does this oxygen frighten you?"

"No." Philippe kissed him on both cheeks before Raoul caught him back in his arms. "There's a girl at my school named Talitha. She's from California and has to wear oxygen all the time. It's because of the altitude." Raoul didn't know that. "Does that needle in your arm hurt you?"

"Nah. I can't even feel it."

"What's it for?"

"To give me food."

"Why don't you just eat?"

Raoul hadn't heard a laugh come out of his father in ages. Certainly not one that hearty. "I haven't been hungry."

"We had chicken nuggets today," Philippe mentioned. "Uncle Raoul would go get you some." He looked at Raoul with imploring eyes. "He'd like them."

"I'm sure he would." Raoul was trying to keep a straight face, but Crystal had already burst out laughing. It drew his father's attention.

"Ah, Crystal. It's been such a long time."

"Too long," she agreed and bent over to kiss his cheeks. "I'm sorry you've been ill."

"It's nothing. Have you come for Christmas?" The hope in his voice caused Raoul to hold his breath.

"Yes. Philippe and I didn't want to spend this one away from you and Arlette."

"Did you hear that, *mon amour?*"

There was new animation in his voice. Raoul's mother nodded and leaned over to kiss his father's forehead. "I certainly did. That's why you've got to get better quick!"

Suddenly Philippe pulled something out of his parka pocket and leaned over to put it in his grandfather's hand.

He lifted it with his free arm. "What's this?"

"*Père Noël. Grand-mère* let me take him off the tree. I asked him to make you all better. You can keep him until you come home. Then I'll put him in my spy kit."

"You have a spy kit?"

"Yes."

"I want to see it."

"It has lots of cool stuff you'd like."

Raoul sensed another miracle was happening. When he lifted his eyes to thank Crystal, he discovered her struggling to ward off her tears. The first miracle was that she'd come back to France with him.

The wall she'd slowly erected months before Eric had been killed had been so high, he hadn't expected her capitulation. If it weren't for Philippe...

CHAPTER THREE

CRYSTAL CLIMBED IN the backseat with Philippe while Arlette sat in the front seat with Raoul for the drive back to the chalet. The short drive only took five minutes. After seeing Jules's reaction, everyone was in higher spirits, but Crystal feared the surprise might have been too much and had drained his strength.

"Stop fretting, Crystal. You and Philippe were just what the doctor ordered," Raoul said. He'd glanced at her several times through the rearview mirror, reading her mind.

"How soon can he come home?"

Arlette turned her head toward Philippe. "That's up to the doctor to decide, but if I know your grandfather, he wants to come home tomorrow."

"I wish he could."

"So do I, but since he can't, I have a surprise for you."

"What is it?"

"You'll find out as soon as we reach the house."

There was another car in the drive when Raoul stopped the car. Before everyone got out, Vivige appeared on the front porch with her children.

"There's Albert. Hooray!"

The two older brunettes, Fleur and Lise, nine and ten respectively, followed Vivige, who hurried down the steps to hug Crystal while Philippe got reacquainted with towheaded Albert. They all started to go in the house, but Crystal noticed that Raoul didn't join them.

Philippe turned to him. "Come on, Uncle Raoul!"

"I'll be back later when it's time for dinner."

"But I don't want you to go."

"Philippe—" Crystal put her hands on his shoulders. "He hasn't even been home yet or seen his girlfriend." If she kept saying it long enough, maybe she'd be able to handle it. She would have to if she were to acquire a new sister-in-law down the road. "We'll talk to him later, honey. Don't forget your cousins are waiting."

"Okay." He kicked at the snow with his boot. "Promise you'll come back?" Philippe had enjoyed his uncle's exclusive attention since his arrival in Breckenridge. It was hard for him to give it up, even for a short while.

"Bien sûr. Ciao."

Philippe must have remembered that word because his cute little face brightened. *"Ciao."*

Everyone hurried through the house into the kitchen for cocoa and the special cookies Vivige made at Christmas for the kids. All the distractions made the time pass quickly. Crystal got them settled in and helped with dinner. As they were finishing their dessert, Raoul entered the dining room.

She looked up, expecting that he'd brought his girlfriend. Crystal had been dreading it, but to her relief he'd come alone. She could tell he'd showered and shaved. In wool slacks and a navy sweater with a wide white stripe, his male appeal overwhelmed her.

His gaze took in everyone before leveling on her. "Sorry I'm late, but I had a small crisis to attend to at work." Most likely he'd been with Sylvie Beliveau and had forgotten the time.

"Sit next to Mom." Philippe's suggestion took Crystal by surprise when there were two other empty seats. After he complied, her son said, "Uncle Bernard called our dessert *les pets de nonne.* Why did everyone laugh?"

Raoul's lips twitched. "Well, nuns sometimes make noises just like other people."

"You mean burps?"

"That and other things."

In a second Philippe figured it out and laughed so hard it made everyone laugh. Vivige stood up from the table. "Come on, everyone. We'll play a game in the other room and let Uncle Raoul finish his dinner in peace. Then we have to go home because you have school in the morning."

The children gave a collective groan.

Crystal appreciated the change of subject and the exodus. Once they were left alone she told him what his sister had brought up earlier about Philippe possibly attending school with Albert.

"She said it was your idea, Raoul. I think it's wonderful. While things are so rocky with your father, it would be good if Philippe's in school so I can be a support to your mother. If you suggested it, he just might go along with it."

He finished the rest of his coffee. "It's worth a try. If he's willing, why don't I come by in the morning and pick up the two of you. We'll drive to the school and talk to Albert's teacher. If she's in agreement, we'll see how it goes. If he starts feeling too insecure, they can call me and we'll go pick him up."

She drew in a deep breath. "You're a good man, Raoul Broussard." *Just keep thinking of him as a good man, Crystal. Your brother-in-law. Someone else's boyfriend. Nothing else.*

"That remains to be seen. Let's take him upstairs now and talk to him. I think you need bed as much as he does."

His remark didn't require a comment. Crystal imagined she'd never looked worse. She got up from the table and followed him to the salon. Fleur was declared the winner of charades and good-nights were said.

Raoul grabbed Philippe and put him on his shoulders. Crystal trailed them and heard her son whoop it up all the way to the bedroom where he dove onto the double bed. He lay there looking up at his uncle. "Can Mom and I come over to your house tomorrow?"

No-o, Philippe.

"You can after I get home from work, but there's something I'd like you to do for me first."

"What?"

"Albert is very happy you're here and he wants you to go to school with him tomorrow."

"School?" Philippe looked like he'd never heard of it.

"It might be fun to see what it's like here."

He blinked. "Do I have to go?"

"No, honey," Crystal said. "It's your choice. But if you stay home, you can't go over to your uncle's until he's through with his work."

The wheels were turning. "Do you think Albert's teacher is mean?"

Raoul chuckled. "Not that I've heard. You could go tomorrow and find out."

"I'll go with you, honey. If you're unhappy, the school will call and I'll come and get you. But you'll have to do your part and be good while you sit next to your cousin. Think about it and you can tell me in the morning. Now it's time for your bath."

"Okay." He got off the bed. "Are you going home now, Uncle Raoul?"

"Just as soon as I look in on your grandfather one more time." Raoul gave him a hug, then flashed her a glance. "If I don't hear from you in the morning, then I'll be by at quarter to eight."

She walked him out to the hallway away from her son, who'd disappeared into the en suite bathroom. "I'm indebted to you for taking such wonderful care of me and Philippe. He needed this trip and it's obvious your father needs him. I want him to get well and I'll do whatever I can to help make it happen. But I don't want Philippe to become a burden to you while we're here."

His dark brows knit together. "A burden...Philippe?"

Her pulse sped up. "You know what I mean. You're his favorite person. He'd spend every moment with you if he could."

"The feeling's mutual."

"But Sylvie—is it?—might not like having to share you with him."

He stared at her long and hard. "Sounds like Vivige has been doing some talking, but despite her wishful thinking, that relationship never got off the ground."

To Crystal's consternation, her first reaction was one of fierce relief. "I'm sorry I said anything. She happened to mention it because—"

"Because the family still worries about me," he interrupted. "The only person who's important right now is Philippe. I happen to love that child." His jaw hardened. "On the way to the hospital the day you went into labor, you both almost lost your lives. That's not something I'll forget."

"Neither will I," she whispered.

"If you're about to tell me to keep my distance, it's too late for that."

"I didn't mean—"

"Oh, yes, you did," he added in a wintry tone. "But I've learned through bitter experience that feelings have a life of their own and come to the surface whether we like it or not. Philippe's too young and innocent to know about that yet. He just does what comes naturally from the sweetness in his nature. Let's pray he never loses that gift."

He wheeled around and strode swiftly down the hall toward the stairs. She hadn't meant to upset him and ran after him. "Please don't go yet. Please—" she begged.

Her cry caused him to pause at the top step. "We're both exhausted, Crystal." His drawn features verified his words. She thought he was about to say something else, then thought the better of it. "Get a good night's sleep. We'll talk tomorrow when you're up to hearing the list of your son's grievances."

She gripped the top of the cutwork wooden balcony until her knuckles grew white. "Why didn't he tell *me?*"

Raoul had already reached the bottom step. He looked up. "That's easy. He loves you too much to hurt you. If he were to do that, then his whole world would collapse. Don't you think it's time you stopped punishing him for something that's not his fault?"

Crystal stood there long after he'd disappeared. Raoul's question had reached down inside her core and had exposed her to herself, forcing her to face an important truth. She'd been feeling so guilty about not loving Eric anymore, she'd become too self-reliant. In the process, she hadn't realized how it was affecting Philippe, but she knew it now.

With their dark blond hair and Broussard features, Philippe and Albert could almost pass for brothers and were close to the same height. They looked so cute sitting in Albert's class at the same table with two classmates.

Being a year younger than the others, Philippe had his pride to consider. Crystal felt that would be the reason he made it through the day, *if* he could last that long.

She stood next to Raoul in the open doorway to the school room as if they were his parents. It should have been Eric standing there with her, but life wasn't fair and it hadn't turned out that way, depriving Philippe of a father.

Her eyes smarted as she watched the teacher welcome Albert's cousin to class. When the introductions were over, Philippe looked back at them with a little smile and gave them a wave.

Another smile. She'd seen more of them since his uncle had turned up than she'd seen in a whole year.

"We'd better go before I burst into tears." She started down the hall toward the exit. "I feel like this is his first day of school."

"At a French school anyway," Raoul murmured as he opened the front door for them. "We'll go back to my house for something to eat while we talk." He cupped her elbow to help walk her to the car so she wouldn't slip on the snow. The gesture was automatic to him, but she was acutely aware of his touch no matter how hard she tried not to think about it.

He lived in Les Pecles near his parents' home in a smaller, more modern chalet with exposed beams. She'd been welcomed into his house many times as his sister-in-law, but today she was plagued by fear to be alone with him.

Never in his life had he done anything to make her feel uncomfortable. It was an old primitive fear all on her part that had come on a month before Eric's death. She could still remember the moment when Philippe had been waiting for his daddy to come home so they could play together. But her husband had forgotten his promise in a long string of unkept promises.

While her son was in tears out in front pulling his little red wagon around, Raoul happened to pull up to the condo and had caught both of them in a vulnerable moment. When he'd put an arm around them to give comfort, a feeling had crept through her that was so far from being sisterly, she'd come close to fainting.

The revelation filled her with such tremendous guilt and shame, it made her ill. She'd suffered a headache for days afterward.

From then on she was so horrified by her attraction to Raoul, she'd begged Eric to reconsider moving.

If not Breckenridge, then somewhere else in Europe where he could train for part of the year. She'd used all her powers of reasoning and persuasion, but he wouldn't budge on the subject and told her to leave it alone.

After his death, she'd wanted to leave for Colorado immediately, but the whole family insisted she stay. They needed her and Philippe, and she needed them. It was true, except that she could see Philippe clinging to his uncle all the time. With the paparazzi around taking pictures of the Broussards at every opportunity, speculation always abounded. She had to end it because Raoul wasn't his father.

And there was more to it than that. Raoul had been seeing other women. One day he'd fall in love again and get married. For Philippe to get any more attached and then have to fight for his uncle's attention with a new aunt would spell more heartache for her son, who'd been through enough losing his father.

Determined to spare him that, she'd found the strength to leave Chamonix before Christmas. She was convinced Philippe would thrive around her family. It had been the right thing to do for all their sakes, or so she'd thought. Now here they were, back again, and she was terrified by her feelings that had only gained in strength after seeing him again.

Once Raoul helped her in the car she said, "Let's eat at the Château des Enfants. It's right here in Les Mouilles. In case we get a call from the school, we can come right back." She'd thrown out the first idea to enter her head. Going on to his house would not be a good idea.

"If that's what you'd prefer." His response eased

her anxiety. "But I'm prepared to wager Philippe will stick it out."

"Maybe." She stared straight ahead. "Do you have any news about Jules this morning?"

"I talked to the nurse a little while ago. She said he had the best night's sleep he's had since being admitted and his blood pressure was down."

"That's marvelous news. I'm so thankful."

"We all are. My mother's going to stay with him most of the day." He drove them the few blocks it took to reach the quaint café full of skiers and tourists. Crystal had eaten here many times with the children. It was a great place for snacks and hot drinks close to Vivige's house. Noisy. *Safe*.

Raoul found a table for them in the back and put in an order for bread and honey with a pot of hot chocolate. "After school we'll take Philippe and Albert over to see him."

"You have more faith that Philippe will last the whole day than I do." She finally lifted her eyes to him. She found his scrutiny unnerving. "Don't think I don't appreciate everything you've done for us, but I'm worried about you. Don't you need to be at work? After flying to the States and back, you probably have a dozen fires to put out."

"The staff has handled every crisis, leaving me free to take care of my family. I'll drop in there sometime today." His calm demeanor managed to unsettle her nerves even more. Crystal didn't know how much longer she could take being alone with him like this, not when she was enjoying it too much.

"Now that Philippe isn't with us, I'm ready to hear that list of grievances you told me about."

After their food was served he said, "Do I really have to spell it out for you when we both know one word would cover it?"

Heat swamped her cheeks.

Raoul leaned forward. "He's been homesick. Whether you want to believe it or not, you raised a little French boy. Every time I talked to him on the phone, he cried that he wanted to go home. There were times when he begged me to come and get him, not because he didn't love you, but because you refused to take him."

She bit her lip so hard, she was surprised it didn't draw blood. "But Eric isn't here."

A strange quiet surrounded Raoul. "No, he's not."

Feeling more tongue-tied than ever she said, "I'm hoping that by the time we go home after Christmas, your father will be better and it won't be nearly so hard for Philippe because he'll realize that what he'd really wanted to come here for was gone."

Except that wasn't true and they both knew it. Philippe loved his French family and worshipped his uncle Raoul. *Far too much.*

She poured honey on her bread and began eating. To her dismay her emotions were in such chaos, she couldn't taste anything. On the other hand Raoul had finished off his bread and hot chocolate in no time at all.

"Don't be surprised if Breckenridge never feels like home to him, Crystal."

Ready for that she said, "But it's *my* home." Raoul had no idea she was fighting for her life. "When we leave Chamonix this time, I'll make a promise to bring him back during his spring recess. That will help make another separation less painful."

His dark blue eyes impaled her. "You think?" He suddenly pushed himself away from the table and stood up, sending out shock waves that assailed her body.

She noticed he'd dressed in a white Scandinavian sweater of primarily blues and gray in the yoke. Between that and his attractively disheveled black hair, he drew the eye of every female in the café. Even Crystal, who was struggling not to be aware of him, could see that no male in Chamonix, let alone France, came close in comparison.

"Come on. I'll take you to the house on my way to work."

No. No more togetherness right now.

"Thank you, Raoul, but I think I'll stay here and have another cup of hot chocolate. After that, I'm going to do some serious Christmas shopping."

She heard his sharp intake of breath. "You're sure? Jet lag will probably catch up with you."

Crystal had never been more sure of anything. "Yes. I gave the secretary at the school my cell phone number, too. If there's a problem, I'll be close by. If all goes well, then I'll meet you at the school at three."

After a noticeable silence he said, *"Bon."*

She forced herself not to stare at him as he put down money and left the café. Once his tall, dark figure had disappeared, she poured herself another drink, then looked up the nearest car rental on her phone.

Raoul would have lent her a car from the business in a second, but she didn't want any more favors from him. She needed to be independent this trip. Before leaving Chamonix she'd given Eric's family the sports car. She had no idea what they'd done with it. As for their Peugeot, she'd sold it in order to buy another car for her and Philippe after they reached Breckenridge.

At first the man at the rental car place told her there were none available right now because of Christmas. But when he heard the name Broussard, magic happened. Within ten minutes a driver pulled up in front of the café and drove her to the rental agency.

She was touched that all the employees working there offered their condolences about Eric and asked for her autograph. One of the cute younger men said, "Are you here to do some racing?" His eyes danced.

"Not this time."

"I like to ski, but I need to perfect my technique. Maybe the great Crystal Broussard could give me a few lessons? I'm off day after tomorrow. I would be the envy of every man in the valley. Please tell me you'll say yes."

He was hitting on her, but he was nice and it built her confidence. After the way Eric had forgotten she'd been a skier, too, this man's attention was a balm to the loss of her self-esteem.

"I won't be skiing this holiday, but you're very kind to ask. Maybe another time."

She signed on the dotted line for the car and drove away, thinking hard about the guy who'd asked her for a ski lesson. If the truth be told, while he'd been flirting with her, she'd wished it had been Raoul. But that had to remain her secret.

As for the rental car guy, he'd actually given her an idea. Provided Jules kept improving, she might just do some skiing tomorrow morning after she dropped

Philippe off at school. It was hard to believe she hadn't been on skis since Eric's death.

For the next few hours she went in and out of the darling shops for children and bought toys she knew Philippe would love. When they went home she would have to buy another suitcase just to get everything back to Breckenridge, but she couldn't resist the items you could never find in the States.

Another day she'd take Philippe shopping. Together they'd pick out gifts for the cousins and family, but today was the perfect time to get his. She'd keep them hidden in the trunk and he'd never know. When he was asleep, she'd smuggle them into the house.

She arrived back at the school at quarter to three, surprised there'd been no call yet. Eager to know how his day had gone, she slipped inside the building and stood outside the door to his room.

The children were doing their maths. Philippe's blond head was bent over the desk while he wrote, reminding her of Schroeder, the little boy bent over his piano playing Beethoven in the Charlie Brown cartoon. The thought brought a smile to her face.

"Looks like your son is thriving."

Raoul. She felt his warmth. "Yes," she said without looking at him.

"All that worry for nothing."

The bell rang, preventing her from having to answer because the children shouted in happiness and came charging out of the room. Philippe flew into her arms. "The teacher said I could come all the time!"

With those words it meant he wanted to be at school with Albert. His homesickness was cured simply by being back. "That's wonderful, honey."

In the next breath she hugged Albert. "Thank you for being such a good friend to him."

"It was fun. The teacher asked him to help us with our English. When he told us the name of his favorite dessert in English, the class laughed their heads off."

Raoul grinned. "The Americans have their funny names for food, too." When Crystal looked at him, his eyes were laughing, filling a dark space inside her. After the way he'd left the café earlier, she didn't think it was possible. "You'll have to tell that story to *Grand-père*. Let's go see him. I happen to know he's waiting for you two."

Taking a fortifying breath, Crystal went down the hall and out the door with the three of them. When they reached the car, she said, "You guys go with Uncle Raoul. I'll follow in my car."

Philippe's eyes grew huge. "You bought a new car?"

"No, honey. It's a rental to use while we're here. See you in a few minutes." She kept walking toward the red car, not wanting to witness Raoul's reaction.

He'd been waiting on her and Philippe for too long. Eric was gone now and things had changed. Arranging for a rental car made the statement that Raoul didn't have to take care of her anymore. That was how she wanted it.

The boys waved to her en route to the hospital. Albert was the blessing Philippe needed right now. He provided the companionship her son had been denying himself.

When they reached the hospital and the boys crowded around their *grand-père's* bed, she could see they were a blessing to Jules too. He was delighted to see them and laughed when they told him all about their day at school.

The best news was that he no longer wore an oxygen tube and was propped up eating some broth. She glanced at Raoul, who didn't look as worried as before. The signs of recovery couldn't be better.

Suddenly he caught her staring at him. His eyes spoke for him. She felt his chastisement. *You should never have left. See what coming back with me has done for him?*

Yes, she saw. She also sensed he wasn't pleased she'd acted on her own to get the rental car, but he had to understand she wanted him to get on with his own life. Crystal had to get on with hers and was doubly thankful she'd rented it. Now she could come and go with Philippe on her own. That way Raoul would have no reason to be on call for them day and night.

After the children had entertained Jules with more stories about school, she gave him a kiss. "My father always told me a good visit was a short one. We're going to leave now so you can rest and get better."

"I'm feeling like a new man."

"That's the best news in the world. When we come back tomorrow, I hope to see you walking around." She squeezed his hand.

"Ciao, Grand-père." Both boys blew him a kiss before they left the room.

Jules's laughter followed them out the door. *"Ciao, mes petits-fils!"* His voice was definitely stronger.

Crystal ushered them from the hospital to Raoul's car. "Say goodbye to Albert, honey. Uncle Raoul's going to drive him home."

He threw his head back to look at her. "But Uncle Raoul said we could go over to his house."

"Not tonight, honey. Your grandmother will have dinner ready and you're going to need an early night if you're going to school again tomorrow."

"But I want us to go with him." The first sign of tears and rebellion all day. "He said we could if I went to school."

"That's true." Raoul's deep voice sounded behind her. "If you can't join us, I'll get him home early."

Crystal remembered that was the deal. "All right." She kissed both boys and waved them off before getting in her car without looking at Raoul.

After she drove home, she put the presents in the storeroom and hurried upstairs. Arlette had dinner waiting. They talked about Jules and Philippe, especially about the hard year he'd had. Right in the middle of their conversation, Philippe came running in the kitchen ahead of Raoul.

She prayed they hadn't heard anything. Her son hurried over to her. "Are you crying?"

"Yes." She smiled and gave him a hug. "We were talking about what a terrific boy you are. That always makes me cry."

"Your mother's right." Arlette reached for him and gave him a kiss. "You've been gone all day and I've missed you. Did you have a good time?"

"Yes. We went skating. Uncle Raoul says I'm awesome."

Crystal rubbed his dark blond head. "That doesn't surprise me. Have you thanked him?"

"Yes." He turned to Raoul. "Didn't I?"

"Several times." She felt his gaze on her. "Maybe next time you'll come with us."

"I'd love it."

Since coming back to Chamonix, she'd made a resolution to be more active with her son instead of taking a backseat. If it meant being with Raoul in the process while they were here, then she'd do it. She didn't want Philippe thinking she was purposely avoiding his uncle.

Christmas would be here soon. Hopefully her father-in-law would be well enough by then that she could take Philippe back to Breckenridge and start a new year free of pain. With the understanding that they would come again in the spring, she was counting on her son not having a complete meltdown.

She turned to Raoul. "Thanks again for being the greatest uncle on earth, as Philippe always says. Now it's time for a young man I know to get ready for bed. I'll go upstairs and start your bath. Say good-night to everyone."

After leaving Crystal, Raoul drove on home. He pulled off his boots and opened the fridge for a beer, but he was out. Not wanting anything else, he shut the door and wandered into the living room without turning on the lights.

At night he often left them off to enjoy the natural snowscape outside his window. Though he'd lived here all his life, the scenery always blew his mind. It reminded him of those deeply crevassed glaciers of the Himalayas, only these glaciers angled toward the Chamonix valley from Mont Blanc.

Tonight the vista reminded him of his earlier conversation with Philippe. When he'd brought his nephew home for dinner, Philippe had pointed to it. "I think that mountain looks like a king with a huge crown of ice on his head. Don't you?"

Raoul had squeezed his shoulder. "That's exactly how it looks." He glanced down at the boy who noticed everything and had a reverence for nature. Somehow without him realizing it, Philippe had climbed into his heart a long time ago and had taken up residence.

"How come you don't have a tree yet?"

"I was waiting for you to come. Day after tomorrow I'll be free and we'll go find one. You can make some decorations for it. How does that sound?" He hadn't had the Christmas spirit for years.

The boy rested his blond head against Raoul. With a sigh he said, "I wish Mommy and I could live with you all the time and never have to go away."

In that instant, those words had wrapped Raoul in their sweet tentacles and wouldn't let him go.

"I'd like the same thing," he whispered in a moment of truth. Deep down he'd wanted it for a long time, but had fought it with everything in him.

Philippe lifted hopeful blue eyes to him. "Please, will you ask Mommy? She'll listen to you."

Raoul's body gave up a shudder. He couldn't believe he'd just said those words aloud in front of Philippe. It was like lighting a fuse. "I wish it were that simple, *mon gamin,* but I'm not your daddy." As Crystal had said, *But Eric isn't here.* Had she said it thinking of Philippe's feelings, or had she expressed them for her own sake? That was the question he needed to have answered.

"I don't care," Philippe answered right back.

"Talitha's mommy lives with her boyfriend and he's not her daddy."

"The girl on oxygen?"

"Yup."

He looked down at Philippe. "Did her daddy die?"

"She doesn't have a daddy."

Out of the mouths of babes. "I thought you didn't make any friends at your school."

"Talitha's not my friend. I heard some kids talk about her."

Raoul's heart thundered in his chest. He was in such deep water already, he didn't dare let this subject continue. "Come on. Let's put your parka on so we can go ice skating. We'll have to hurry since you've got school in the morning."

All along he'd planned to drive Philippe to school every day. It would give him an excuse to be with Crystal, who never lighted long enough for them to have an in-depth conversation. Unfortunately her move to get a rental car had thrown him, but it didn't change his intention of being there for his nephew. If she didn't like it, that was too bad. Philippe wanted and expected to be with him now that he was here.

Like a wound that had been torn open again, his conversation with Philippe had brought all his agony to the surface, leaving him bleeding all over the place. He needed to do something about his turmoil or he honestly didn't know how he was going to make it through the night, let alone the rest of his life.

CHAPTER FOUR

AFTER DROPPING Philippe off at school the next morning, Crystal drove to Broussard's and parked around the side entrance reserved for the staff. The famous mountaineering shop looked like a giant chalet and catered to everything for the mountain climber, but it also carried ski clothes and equipment. Raoul's office was on the third level at the other end. As she walked through the lower level to the ski shop, she doubted he was even at work yet.

"*Eh bien*—I can't believe my eyes."

She smiled. "*Bonjour,* Jean-Luc."

The ski veteran who'd run the shop for years came around the counter and gave her a bear hug. "If it isn't Crystal, as I live and breathe. You are a sight for sore eyes."

"It's great to see you, too." He was like family to the Broussards. Jean-Luc had been a fabulous skier in his time and had given Eric a lot of pointers.

"What brings you in here?"

"I want to rent some equipment to go up skiing for a couple of hours."

His brows lifted. "You didn't bring your own gear?"

"Not this time. This was a spur-of-the-moment

decision." Thanks to Raoul, who'd infused her with the determination to get back doing what she did best.

"Well…let me fix you up. I'm afraid we don't have your special skis, but I think I can find something for the famous Colorado champion."

Before long she was outfitted with ski bibs and everything she'd need. He found an empty dressing room for her to change in and let her put her things in a locker in the back room.

Once she was ready, she put her skis and poles over her shoulder and started for the same side entrance. It was only a short walk to the Brévent cable car.

But she never made it outside because a tall, powerfully built man in a familiar black bomber jacket was just coming in, blocking her exit. She looked up at him and trembled. "Raoul—"

His hands shot out to grip her upper arms. At his touch, a jolt of electricity arced through her body. "I saw your rental car out there as I was driving around to the back." She felt his gaze travel over her like a laser beam. "Give me a minute to get into my ski gear and I'll go up to Planpraz with you. I haven't had a good run on skis in weeks."

Warmth flooded her system. It wasn't just his physical presence that made it difficult to catch her breath. It was the fact that he was willing to drop everything to come with her. She'd always loved that trait in Raoul. His spontaneity at a moment's notice made him such an exciting man to be with. Though it was taking an emotional risk, for once she didn't question it because the negative tension between them seemed to be missing.

"I'll wait outside the door for you." Maybe it was

the day, the air. All she knew was, she wanted to be with him.

His hands fell away, leaving her free to continue walking, but her legs felt like mush. If this was the way he was going to affect her, she didn't think she had the strength to make it to the cable car, let alone ski. He was a wonderful skier and an even more wonderful companion when he was relaxed. Thrill after thrill darted through her at the thought of being with him like this.

She didn't have to wait long before he joined her looking fantastic in his black ski outfit with the blue stripe up the side. They walked the short distance to the ski station in companionable silence before riding the cable car up the mountain. Soon Chamonix lay at their feet. She gasped softly at the phenomenal sight while experiencing an attack of exhilaration that she was seeing this with him.

This was her world! For a few years she'd forgotten. When she turned her head, her eyes fused with the cobalt blue of Raoul's.

"You've got that look on your face, Crystal."

"What look is that?" she whispered shakily.

"The one that used to be on all the billboards. The look that's been missing. I'm glad to see it's back. I'll race you to the bottom." His gaze reluctantly left hers before he gripped his poles and started down the run, exploding like a torpedo out of its silo past two other skiers.

She adjusted her goggles and pushed off, eager to catch up to him. They played like children, skiing the moguls down the steep piste. Sheer euphoria. She let out a joyous laugh and poured on the speed, flying past him. She eventually reached the bottom a few seconds faster than he did.

Crystal was still laughing for the utter pleasure of being alive and sharing this with him. When he skied over to her, his smile dissolved her bones. "You're still the greatest thing going out here. If anything, I think you're skiing better than you used to. You were loose. Fluid."

Raoul. "You're good for my ego."

"I think you meant that." His expression grew more thoughtful. "How about one more run before I have to get a little work done today?"

"You're on!" she cried, delirious with happiness that he wanted to go again.

They skied over to the station and rode the cable car once more. It filled up fast. Raoul's intense gaze found hers over the heads of the other skiers. His gorgeous eyes conveyed so many things, she felt giddy.

Their second run was even more exciting because Raoul was determined to win. And she let him.

He flashed her a crooked half smile while he waited for her to ski over to him. She hadn't fooled him, of course. "Thanks for making a mediocre skier look like a pro in front of our audience. I owe you for that." A small crowd had gathered to watch them.

She chuckled. "I've had the time of my life this morning." For once she'd done something for pure pleasure. No cross examinations, no guilt she was trying to hide. She'd just gone with the moment because Raoul had made her feel so good.

"My sentiments exactly," he said in his deep voice. It sent delicious chills through her body. She sensed this had been good for him, too.

They removed their skis and started walking back to his work, cocooned in their own world for the moment by the spell holding them after such a fabulous morning. Halfway there, Raoul's cell phone rang. He had to pick up. When his black brows furrowed, she had to accept the fact that reality had intruded.

After he'd taken the call, his glance swerved to hers. "I've got a situation I have to deal with immediately."

Inside she moaned. "You go on."

"I'll be in touch with you later."

He took off like a shot through the crowd of skiers. A guide had probably called in because of an emergency. Raoul was always the first to respond and coordinate any mountain rescue efforts. She hoped he didn't have to go himself. There was always a certain amount of danger, but after being with him this morning, her normal worry for him escalated to new heights.

She returned to the chalet and changed back into her street clothes. After thanking Jean-Luc, she left to get some lunch and do a little more Christmas shopping. Pretty soon it was time to pick up Philippe.

Crystal spotted him right away. For his second day at school he'd chosen to put on his dark blue pants and lighter blue polo shirt with the long sleeves. It wasn't like Albert's uniform, but Crystal could see the colors were close enough.

"Guess what, Mommy?" He'd just come out of the room with his cousin. "I'm in the school program, too. We're going to be Christmas angels."

"You are? How exciting!" She walked them to the car and they got in. "When is it?"

"On Saturday afternoon. We have to sing two songs."

"Just you and Albert?"

"All the kids," her nephew said.

"Which Christmas carols are they?"

"I don't know. Uncle Raoul will help me practice."

She looked at him through the rearview mirror. "We'll get Aunt Vivige to teach you since she'll know the songs Albert is working on."

"But I want *him* to do it."

"Honey, he doesn't have the time."

"He'll help if I ask him."

"I'd rather you didn't." She felt she was going under for the third time. Though her morning with Raoul had been magical, it had to end.

"You're mean."

"What did you say to me?"

"I'm sorry." Here came the tears. While he sat there crying hysterically, there was a knock on the rear window causing both their heads to turn. It was Raoul.

She was elated to realize that he wasn't out on an emergency, but she was surprised to see him here. Philippe unstrapped himself and scrambled out of the backseat into his arms where he sobbed even harder.

"*Eh, bien,* what's wrong, *mon gars?* Do you feel sick today?" Anyone nearby would assume Raoul was the father attempting to console his son. The love he had for Philippe had always been the real thing and it was reciprocated a hundred fold.

Crystal had known fear once before around Raoul. Now she felt it even stronger to see the way Philippe clung to him. This affection for his uncle that had its roots deep in the past was reaching critical mass. With a sense of despair, she knew it would only grow stronger. She needed some advice about now.

His cute little face was all blotchy. "Mommy says you don't have time to t-teach me some s-songs for the school program."

"Of course I do." Raoul turned his dark head in her direction. "Did you hear that, Mommy?" Raoul had turned his back on her, reminding her of their conversation outside the bedroom the other night when he'd told her Philippe could never be a burden.

This was so hard. Crystal resented being in the position of the enemy when Philippe was her son. But this wasn't a situation where blame could be attached to any one person. Whatever she said right now would spell the difference between temporary peace or permanent chaos. It wouldn't be fair to create more problems when Jules wasn't even out of the hospital yet.

"I did. I just didn't know if it was all right with you, Raoul."

Crystal thought she saw a look of satisfaction enter Raoul's eyes before he kissed his forehead. "There. Did you hear that?" Philippe nodded. "Have a treat on me." Raoul pulled two small wrapped candy canes from his pocket and undid them for the boys.

Philippe put it in his mouth. "Mmm. This tastes good, like peppermint."

"Yum," Albert said.

"I brought them especially for you guys because I know you like that flavor."

"Thanks!"

"You're welcome." Though he was speaking to the boys, his focus was on Crystal. After taking in her knitted blue ski hat, Raoul's eyes narrowed on her mouth. Fire ran through her body, igniting her. It brought back the joy she'd shared with him earlier.

Maybe it was the cream-colored cable knit pullover he was wearing that made his eyes look inky blue in the afternoon light. Helpless to do otherwise, her gaze lowered to the jeans molding his powerful thighs. Her heart thumped hard as she took in his features again. To think any one man could be that handsome…

Out of the corner of her eye she saw Vivige pull up. Her daughters rushed toward her car. More than ever it didn't explain Raoul's presence. The thought—the hope that after this morning's ski run he might be missing Crystal's company—gave her a suffocating feeling in her chest.

Vivige opened her window. "Come on, Philippe, Albert," she called to them. "We're off to the hospital to see *Grand-père*." The boys scrambled into her car. Philippe was perfectly happy again.

"I'll feed the children dinner. See you two later," Vivige murmured as she looked at the two of them.

After she drove off, Raoul's gaze flicked to Crystal. Her pulse was galloping. "I came by here to catch up with you because I want to give you your prize."

She smiled. "My prize? For what?"

His eyes held a mysterious gleam. "For letting me win in front of that crowd earlier."

Crystal laughed. "You're not serious."

"Oh, but I am," he insisted, "and I always pay my debts."

Thump thump went her heart. "Where is it?"

"In town at Chez Pierre. We'll go in my car. I'll bring you back later." He helped her out and they walked back to his car.

Before long they arrived at the charming bistro, one of many lining the streets of Chamonix. Chez Pierre was known for serving the best cheese fondue in town. The host led them upstairs, where there were tables near the window with a superb view of the mountains. But the second they reached the next level, she let out a cry.

On the two walls facing each other were giant-sized colored posters, bigger than life. Above them were banners that read *Vive les Broussards.* One was of Eric in his famous tuck, heading for the finish line that won him his last gold.

The other one showed Crystal flying down the icy trek with her body perfectly aligned. She wore a smile beneath her ski goggles as she was coming in to take the bronze. Seeing herself at the height of her career in competition form was too much.

In front of the other people eating, she burst into quiet tears. Raoul slid his arms around her and pulled her close to him until she could get hold of herself. Crystal was so moved by his gift, she couldn't find words.

"I didn't bribe Pierre to put up that poster of you, *ma belle.* He's had these in here forever," Raoul whispered. His lips brushed her cheek, sending rivulets of longing through her body. "I wanted to bring you here before you left for the States. But it wasn't meant to be then. It's a testament to a world that still honors Chamonix's best. That's you."

Overwhelmed by this incredible man, she kissed his jaw. "Thank you for believing in me." After she eased out of his arms, he found them a table at the window. It had been reserved for Raoul Broussard.

Her heart jumped to think he'd planned all this. It

was the most romantic, thrilling thing anyone had ever done for her.

Crystal never imagined the day would come when she'd be eating fondue with him like this while she soaked in the atmosphere he'd created by simply being Raoul. But as she ate the French bread she dipped in the bubbling mixture of Gruyère cheese and kirsch, she sensed something was on his mind. She couldn't bear for anything to be wrong right now.

"What is it, Raoul?"

His eyes searched hers. "Did I make a mistake bringing you here?"

"Mistake?" she murmured in shock.

He cocked his dark head. "You're so quiet, I couldn't help wondering."

"Wondering what?"

"Whether my good intentions backfired because seeing Eric's picture here was too much for you."

After what she'd experienced with Raoul today, she couldn't hold back certain information from him. "Before we leave here, there's something you need to know about Eric and me."

"What? That he betrayed you?" he bit out.

Whoa. Where had that come from?

"No—" she answered honestly.

"He had a reputation with women before he married you."

Raoul had never gotten this personal with her before; but since this morning, everything seemed to have changed.

"I know. My teammates warned me about him. He was known as the heartbreaker on the circuit, but I couldn't help how I felt about him. We both had the same drive and the same daring, I guess. One day when he said, 'Let's get married right now,' I just went with it."

Shadows marred his features. "Then if it wasn't another woman, what changed in your marriage?"

Crystal let out a shaky breath. "Was it that visible to everyone?"

"No," he said quietly. "Only to me because Eric was my brother. It's something I've never discussed with anyone."

She put down her fondue fork. "You could say the existence of Philippe transformed my life. Until I discovered I was pregnant, I was selfish and didn't think much about anything beyond Eric's and my dreams of success. We were two people flying high and enjoying every minute.

"It pains me now to think we just went off and got married in Val d'Isère without telling either of our families. We cheated everyone out of one of the most important times in all our lives, but Eric insisted we didn't have time for wedding plans and still make all our races."

"Patience was never his forte, but it made him the world's greatest skier."

She nodded. "Still, in hindsight, it was extremely selfish of us. I should have insisted on a traditional wedding. Do you realize we didn't even have one picture of us on our wedding day? Nothing to show for the biggest event in our lives. We were only in the *mairie* ten minutes, and then we were off to our next race in Courchevel so the paparazzi didn't catch on. Sometimes I think about it now and it crushes me."

"But that's absurd," Raoul responded. "No one

cared. The family was thrilled you got married. My parents worried Eric might never settle down. I know your parents were happy. We talked at length about the two stars in our families joining together."

Crystal shook her head. "Two selfish stars. We both agreed to put off having children while we were in our athletic prime, but even with protection, Philippe came along anyway." She took a fortifying breath. "From the moment I became pregnant, my whole outlook on life changed dramatically."

His features took on a chiseled look she didn't understand.

"For once I had to think about someone else besides myself and Eric. The baby's needs superseded everything else. I had to stop skiing, but I didn't mind at all because this miracle of motherhood was going to happen to me. Though Eric was happy we were going to have a baby, he didn't undergo the same transformation."

Raoul's eyes narrowed. "No. My brother developed that killer instinct early to be the top skier in the world. It never left him."

He'd taken the words right out of Crystal's mouth. "No. And at the height of his fabulous winning streak, my new priority was to be the best mother and wife in the world instead of the best female skier. I was determined to make a real home for us. Any hard times came when I saw Eric disappoint our son because he had to be someplace else."

Raoul gave her a commiserating look that spoke of deep understanding.

"Eric went on doing what he was born to do, but our marriage began to suffer because we were on two divergent tracks. I loved him and didn't blame him for who he was any more than he blamed me for my new role of motherhood. But with Philippe's birth, I found out what I was really born to do."

Except that her recent conversation with Raoul reminded her she could have a life off and on the ski slopes, too.

"I tried to salvage our marriage and begged him to move to Breckenridge with me. I thought that if he didn't have your family and friends to depend on all the time, he'd come to rely on me again and we could recapture the love we'd once shared. But he didn't want to leave home."

Raoul wiped the corner of his mouth with his napkin. "My brother was too entrenched."

"Exactly. Eric was too comfortable with the lifestyle he'd known all his life. He couldn't see that he was leaving Philippe alone too much. That drive in him took over and left us behind. I kept hoping things would change, but they didn't. The truth is, though I never said the words to him, if he hadn't been killed, I would have divorced him."

Something flared in the recesses of his eyes. "*That* I didn't know."

"Does it shock you?"

He frowned, staring at her as if he'd never seen her before. "What are you talking about? I loved my brother, but another woman would have left him long before then."

She shook her head. "Even so, forgive me if I sounded disloyal just now."

A strange sound escaped his throat. "I'm the one

asking for forgiveness for sounding judgmental of you the other night about Philippe."

"There's nothing to forgive, Raoul. I *have* been punishing my son unwittingly by pretending I could erase the past." But she'd found out that wasn't possible, and her concern over Philippe's future happiness was looming larger than ever.

She lifted her head. "Thank you for this incredible day. I'll never forget you or your generosity. Now if you wouldn't mind driving me back to the school, I need to get my car and go home so I'll be there when Vivige brings him back."

After dropping Crystal off at her car, Raoul drove home experiencing a new kind of pain. It wasn't like what he'd suffered after Suzanne had died. Her death had been final. He'd had to accept it and get past it through sheer will and work.

But Crystal and Philippe were both breathtakingly alive and, worse, *forbidden* to him in the eyes of society and family. Raoul didn't worry about either, but he knew Crystal did. After experiencing pleasure almost beyond bearing by being with her today, he could see his pain would go on and on with no end in sight unless he did something about it.

Desperate for relief, he reached for his phone and called his best friend. But all he got was his voice mail. Des could be anywhere, doing anything. Raoul left a brief message for him to phone, then hung up.

Desidiero Pastrana, a wealthy Spaniard and mountaineer from the Pyrenees, had arrived in Chamonix ten years ago to do some climbing. Raoul had been his guide and they'd struck up a friendship that had lasted and deepened over the years. They'd often traveled back and forth to do different climbs together, enjoying women until Raoul had met Suzanne.

When she'd been killed, Des had been there for him. They'd done a trip to Nepal that had saved his life. Raoul would always be indebted to him. Now he needed saving again because he was battling excruciating pain that was eating him alive. Des was the only person he could talk to about it.

Though he had a few other good friends, there wasn't anyone else who had Des's depth of character and understanding. He'd been through a hell as real as the one Raoul was going through now. Raoul could benefit from some of his wisdom.

After pacing the floor, he picked up the phone again, this time to call the nursing station at the hospital. The clerk answered. She told him the doctor had made his rounds and had given orders for the feeding tube to be taken out of Monsieur Broussard. He could go on soft foods in the morning.

Dieu, merci. Raoul thanked her and hung up. He'd needed to hear that good news, but it still wasn't enough for him tonight. For once the solitude was killing him and Des might not get back to him for a while.

Unable to stand his own company, he put on his shoes and jacket, then left the house on foot for the nearest bar. He needed something to numb him so he could sleep. Anything at all to help him keep the lid on.

After Crystal left for Breckenridge with Philippe, he'd been in such a black void he'd had no interest in anything except to plunge into his work. That's when he'd started making monthly phone calls to Philippe. It meant he could hear Crystal's voice.

The talks with her son managed to keep him from going insane, but, by October, not even those ended up being enough. Finally one of his colleagues told him he needed to take a break, otherwise he would be no good on the mountain.

After his last unsatisfying few words on the phone with Crystal, he'd been on the verge of phoning her back to tell her he was going to fly to Breckenridge to see his nephew. Then his father had fallen ill and that's when he'd firmed up his decision to go to Colorado and ask her to come back with Philippe.

Though he would never have wished for this scenario, his father's illness had given Raoul the first legitimate excuse he'd been aching for. Ironically, now that Crystal had come, she and Philippe were still untouchable living in his parents' home, and he'd never felt more alone in his life.

Walking faster, he approached the Après-ski Mont Blanc that featured a live band that brought in the crowds. Raoul went inside the lounge and made his way past partying tourists to find an empty table.

Before he could find himself a spot to sit, he felt someone pull on his arm. He turned around. It was a sister of one of the new guides he'd hired. She'd come around the office several times dropping unsubtle hints that said she wished he would ask her out. Hell.

"*Bonsoir,* Monique. You're looking lovely tonight. How are you?"

The brunette smiled. "I'm better now that I've seen you. I had no idea someone like you mixed with a crowd like this. Are you alone?"

He'd thought he'd wanted a drink, but one look in her eyes and he knew he'd been a fool to come in here where he knew he'd be recognized.

"Actually, I was looking for a client wanting to arrange a climb, but don't see him. I guess I kept him waiting too long, so I'll have to catch up with him at the hotel. It's nice to see you again."

"You don't have time for one little dance?"

"I'm sorry, but business has to come first."

She pouted. "That's what Gerard always says."

"Your brother's right. *À bientôt,* Monique."

Raoul had no choice but to leave her standing there. Once out in the cold air, he took a long walk before returning to his house and closing up for the night.

He'd just come out of the shower before going to bed when he heard his phone ring. It could be several people on the other end. Maybe the hospital. He prayed there wasn't an emergency and reached for it. The caller ID indicated it was Des. He clicked on.

"Salut, mon vieux," he said with utter relief.

"Qué tal, Raoul. From what you didn't tell me in your message, I figured you didn't care how late I returned your call."

"You figured right, as usual. How much time have you got?"

"You know better than to ask me a question like that."

He threw on his robe and sank down on the side of the bed. "This goes way back."

"After the hours I've leaned on you over the years when things got tough, I'm more than ready to listen to you."

For the next half hour he unloaded to his good

friend. It was therapeutic to finally let out all his anguish and suffering to someone he trusted.

A long silence followed. "Des?" he prompted at last.

"I've been thinking, *mi gran amigo,* and this is what you have to do." For the next few minutes he laid out what Raoul's instincts had already been telling him to do. He'd just needed corroboration from the man who was like a second brother to him.

"Jules!" Crystal met him in the hall the next afternoon walking with Vivige, who had her arm hooked through his.

"Isn't it *fantastique?*" her sister-in-law cried.

"It certainly is." Crystal hurried toward them and gave him a hug. "What does the doctor say now?"

"I can go home tomorrow provided everything's normal."

"That's the best news I ever heard." They walked back into his hospital room. Crystal helped him get settled in the bed.

Vivige kissed her father. "Now that Crystal's here, I'm going to leave and get some shopping done. I'll see you home tomorrow."

"Wonderful. Now you run along and take care of your family while the two of us have a nice visit."

Once she was out the door, Crystal pulled a chair up to the side of the bed where he was propped. "I like you in that robe."

"*Merci* for buying it for me. I appreciated the flowers your parents sent, too."

"Everyone wants you well, and now you look so much better, I hardly recognize you."

He reached for her hand and squeezed it. "I wish

I could say the same about you." She gulped. "Don't take offense, *ma fille.* You know I'm not talking about your looks. I'm talking about what's inside here." He patted his chest. "Tell me about your plans for the future."

"To take care of Philippe."

His eyes glinted with unshed tears. "He needs a lot of taking care of like any little boy."

Crystal nodded. "You're so right. You ought to know, having raised two yourself."

He gave her a frank stare. "What else?"

Like Raoul, Jules had a direct way of speaking. Since they weren't ones to beat around the bush, she wasn't about to lie to him. "I'm working on some ideas for myself." Raoul had done so much for her confidence, she could never repay him. "But right now I have a lot of angst over Philippe. He's had a rough year."

"That means a doubly rough one for you. I'm sorry." He patted her hand before letting it go. "If I were to tell you time heals all wounds, I'd be a liar. But over the years I've learned time does add perspective, and that makes it possible to pick up again and find joy."

Crystal was thankful she'd had a certain conversation with Raoul yesterday, or she couldn't have handled this one. Suddenly Arlette walked in the room. The timing couldn't have been better.

"The nurse just told me you're going home in the morning." She looked at Crystal. "It's because you came and brought our grandson."

"That and a lot of prayers."

"Raoul insisted on flying to Colorado for you. I'm so grateful he followed his instincts."

Raoul, Raoul.

"I should have come sooner. I'm sorry."

"Don't be." Arlette touched Crystal's cheek. "You weren't ready to deal with anything until now. We understand."

Except that they *didn't* understand this new agony. How could they? Crystal needed to be alone.

"You're the most marvelous in-laws anyone could have. Philippe and I are the lucky ones." Crystal kissed both of them. "I'm going to let you two have this time together while I get more shopping done without a little body knowing what I'm doing."

Both of them smiled. "Will you be home for dinner?"

"Not this evening, Arlette. After school, Philippe's going to help his uncle buy a Christmas tree and decorate it." Since Philippe would blab the news to everyone anyway, there were no secrets. "I'm going to provide the food."

"That sounds delightful."

"Are you going to cook?" Jules asked.

"No. We're having chicken nuggets."

At their horrified expressions, she laughed, but all amusement faded after she left the hospital room.

CHAPTER FIVE

"I bet that's Mommy!"

Raoul's back was against the picture window, where he was hanging the last strand of white lights on the tree. He'd put on a CD of Christmas music both he and Philippe were enjoying. The two songs he had to learn for school were on it. Before the evening was out, he'd have the words memorized.

"Go ahead and open the door for her."

"Okay."

He heard Philippe's excited voice before the two of them came into the living room. His nephew put the food she'd bought on the coffee table.

"Hello," Raoul called out as if they were in the woods.

She glanced across the room and pretended to look for him. "Oh…*there* you are. Hello-o," she called back the same way, making Philippe laugh. As she took off her parka and hat, his heart skipped a beat. The firelight gleamed in the lighter streaks of her blond hair attractively mussed about her face and shoulders. Crystal was a natural beauty.

"For a second I thought you were *Père Noël* hiding behind the pine boughs."

"He's not *Père Noël,* Mommy. You're funny."

"Well, I wasn't sure, not with that deep voice."

"Some day I'll have a deep voice just like his, huh."

"Yes, honey." She moved closer to the fire. "This feels good. It's cold outside."

"It is that," Raoul murmured. Last year she and Philippe had left before Christmas. At that point in time he couldn't have imagined this day.

"Do you like our tree? Uncle Raoul let me pick it out."

"I love it!"

"Can I put on the decorations I made now, Uncle Raoul?"

"Let's do it!"

"Where are they?" she asked.

"On the kitchen table. I'll get them."

"Do you want us to eat in the kitchen, Raoul?"

"No. I think it's more fun by the fire."

"So do I!" Philippe quickly opened one the sacks. "What's this?"

"Grape juice. They didn't have apple."

"Oh." He took a drink. "Mmm. It's good." Then he grabbed a chicken nugget and hurried out of the living room munching on it.

Raoul couldn't help but smile. He'd brought a box out of storage and moved it in front of the tree. "The old ornaments are in here."

Out of the corner of his eye he watched her reach for some and begin hanging them as high up the tree as she could. Her figure did wonders for the stunning outfit she was wearing, a beige sweater toned with cream-colored wool pants.

Philippe came running back in with some drawings

he'd cut into diamond shapes. Raoul had given him a few ornament hangers so he could pierce a hole in the paper.

"Guess what this one is?" Philippe held it up to his mother.

As each ornament was hung carefully on the tree, Crystal and Raoul guessed all the characters he'd drawn from his favorite cartoon show, much to Philippe's delight. As Raoul reached over to take a decoration out of Philippe's hand, he brushed against Crystal's arm accidentally. The contact seared him, and he quickly focused his attention back on Philippe.

"You're a good artist, do you know that?"

"I know. Madame Fillou told me."

"Philippe, you're supposed to say thank you."

"Oh, yeah. Thanks."

Raoul grinned. "You're welcome." In a few minutes they finished decorating the tree. He moved over to the CD player and turned it off. "While your mother and I eat, why don't you impress her and sing the songs you've been learning."

Crystal sat on the couch by him and they began eating. Philippe only needed help here and there. When he'd finished, she clapped her hands. "I'm very proud of you to learn those words so fast."

"So am I," Raoul murmured.

"Thanks." The purple grape juice had stained Philippe's upper lip. Raoul would always retain this picture of him. "Can we sleep here tonight?"

"That's up to your mother."

"Please, Mommy? Uncle Raoul has a pullout bed in the loft where we can play spy."

He felt her body tense. "But we don't have pajamas,

and you don't have a change of clothes for school tomorrow."

"Uncle Raoul bought me and Albert some Bigfoot Monster pajamas and our own toothbrushes for when we sleep over."

"They're a pre-Christmas present," Raoul explained. "Even if you can't stay, I'll run him by the house in the morning to change before I drive him to school."

Crystal nodded her agreement. "Well, aren't you a lucky boy."

Philippe smiled.

Pleased how things were progressing, Raoul got to his feet. "In that case you need to get ready for bed now." He had plans for Crystal once his nephew fell asleep.

"Goody!"

"Give me a kiss good-night, honey."

After hugging his mother, he was off like a shot. Raoul turned to her. "I'll be back down soon."

Raoul must have started a fire early. It was still throwing out heat when Crystal had entered his living room. She never failed to marvel when she walked over to the huge picture window and took in the sight of Mont Blanc. He probably had one of the better views in the whole valley.

Suzanne had made a lovely home for them. Comfy off-white chairs and upholstered sofas were accented by various shades of blue and gray in the slate floors and window seat cushions.

The vaulted ceiling, all in honey wood, crisscrossed with rafters and a wooden cutwork balcony on the second floor, made for a stunning interior. As far as she could tell, Raoul hadn't changed anything.

It was the kind of house that— *No. Don't go there, Crystal.*

"I'm going to make some coffee. Would you like some?"

Lost in her musings, she hadn't realized Raoul had come back downstairs.

"That sounds good. Thank you. Do you think Philippe's asleep?"

"Yes. I just read him a story. He was out like a light before I could finish it."

"That's because he's happy. Raoul, if you don't mind, I'd like to talk to you about something important before I leave."

"I was going to tell you the same thing. I'll be right back with the coffee."

The first part of Raoul's plan to get her alone had just been put in motion. He carried two mugs out to the living room, where he found Crystal studying the pictures on the far wall next to the bookcase. Some were of family, others of his adventures with friends, with Des.

He reached around to hand the coffee to her and felt her body quicken though they weren't touching. She'd reacted that same way once before. It was about a month before Eric died running the piste, but he remembered the moment as clearly as if it had been yesterday.

He'd happened to be in the ski shop with his father while Eric was there talking to Jean-Luc. They were discussing the possibility of his trying out a new boot.

When the secretary buzzed through that there was a call from Eric's wife, he told the secretary he couldn't take it and would call her back later.

The casual way he'd blown her off was a pattern Raoul had noticed for the last year. Though it was none of his business and shouldn't have angered him, it did. Deciding there were too many people in the room, he left work and got in his car. Remembering another call she'd made that had turned out to be an emergency when she'd gone into early labor, he found himself driving over to their condo in a hurry.

Relief swept over him to discover Crystal out in front trying to appease Philippe, who was in tears. He looked so unhappy holding the handle to his little red wagon. Raoul could only assume he'd been waiting for his father. Eric hadn't had a legitimate reason for being away from home that day. He could have at least taken the call.

When Raoul got out of his car, Crystal had looked up at him. The defeated expression in her eyes and body language cut him to the core. Philippe noticed him coming and ran to welcome him. Without conscious thought Raoul picked him up and carried him over to Crystal. He put his arm around her, his only thought to comfort her.

But as he did it, other feelings took hold. He felt the unmistakable rush of desire for his sister-in-law course through him, shocking him to the foundations. She was Eric's wife, yet he wanted her. It was insane. Wrong.

As he was wishing he could go on holding her and never let her out of his arms again, he felt her body give off something he could only describe as a shock wave. He felt it travel through his system and knew in his gut she was aware of what had just happened to him. But to her credit, she went on treating him the same as usual.

With that defining moment of revelation, he'd made a silent vow to keep his distance and had never broken it. But Eric's death changed certain dynamics because Philippe had turned to him, and that meant the three of them were thrown closer together than ever.

From then on, whenever he was around her, he felt like a live wire spitting sparks and knew it was dangerous to be anywhere in her vicinity. When she left for Colorado so abruptly, he realized she was uncomfortable around him.

Up until then she'd been able to shroud her feelings all she wanted with the family and use Philippe for a shield. But today, that particular defense mechanism was no longer working for her.

Shaken again by her reaction to him just now because it might mean what he hoped it meant, Raoul sat down in one of the chairs and stretched out his long legs while he sipped his coffee.

"I have a proposition for you, Crystal." He'd said it to her back. "If you'd sit down, then we could discuss it."

"Proposition?" She turned around with a puzzled look. "If this is about Philippe—"

"It's about both of you," he interrupted before allowing her to finish the sentence.

He noticed shadows beneath her eyes as she sank down on one end of the couch.

She cupped her mug, but didn't drink. "What about us?"

"For the last year I've been hearing the same thing

come out of Philippe every time I've called. He wants to come home. Now that he's here, he doesn't want to leave. It's a fact you can't deny."

She finally swallowed some coffee. "I'm not."

For her to admit it meant another hurdle had been achieved.

"You've already seen that he's taken to going to school with Albert the way you Americans like to say, 'a duck takes to water.' His presence has brought my father back from the brink. I believe he has rejuvenated my parents to the point that I think he's added another twenty years to their lives at least. The cousins are thrilled he's home again. So I have a solution. On the strength of the friendship we've shared over the years, will you hear me out?"

She jumped up from the couch and put the mug on the end table. "I don't need to because I have a solution of my own. As I told you before, I'll bring Philippe to Chamonix several times a year for a visit from now on."

He eyed her steadily. "Then that's a solution for you, not Philippe."

Crystal made a betraying motion with her hand. "He'll adjust in time. He'll have to."

Raoul leaned forward. "Did you know your son thinks you hate it here and that you hate me?" Her color faded a little, letting him know she did. "Is it true?"

Her hands formed fists at her side. "You of all people have to know that nothing could be further from the truth. After yesterday, how can you even ask me such a thing?" Her voice throbbed with feeling, convincing him she'd been as honest as she knew how to be.

They'd got past the second hurdle. Now for the third.

This was the crucial one. If she took the bait, it would tell him he was way off base. That's what he'd told Des and his friend had agreed.

"Then for all our sakes I'd like to see you prove it by coming to work for the family business."

Her translucent blue eyes darkened with some unnamed emotion.

"Eric may not be alive, but you are. I've already told you you're a world-class skiing celebrity in your own right with your own legacy to hand down to Philippe. With him in school full-time, you could devote some of your time to your own ski school here."

"A ski school—"

"Yes. People would flock to classes taught by the one and only famous Crystal Broussard, the Colorado bronze medalist. You could start a brand-new Broussard tradition on your terms and still be a full-time mother to Philippe. It would be the best of both worlds for the two of you."

"You're not serious."

He stood up. "You know I am. You're a former champion and have too much to give to let it all go. If you joined our staff, you'd be given your own office at headquarters and determine your own schedule. You can consider this an official offer, but take your time to think about it. You've got till next year, or didn't you mean what you told Philippe earlier about not going back to Colorado until then."

After a pregnant silence, she said, in a dull voice, "I meant it."

"Then give it some serious thought. You could buy a house here and get your old things out of storage. Several times a year you could fly to Colorado to be with your parents and they could come here. The important thing is that Philippe will have that sense of belonging he's been missing since you left, and you will capitalize on all your years of training."

"That's a very generous offer, Raoul," she said, sounding far away. "I realize other skiers would kill for such an unprecedented opportunity. Have you spoken of this to anyone else?"

"No." Except for Des. "If you decide to do this, then I'll tell Papa, who will be overjoyed, not only from a personal standpoint but a business one. Whatever Philippe intends to do with his life after he's grown up, such a legacy will ensure his future."

His proposal appeared to have put her in more turmoil. He hoped it was tearing her apart. If she turned him down, that would be the answer he was praying for.

"Speaking of your son—" He put his hands on his hips. "I told him we'd all be together after school to welcome his *Grand-père* home. I'll go with *Maman* to bring him back from the hospital."

"I'll pick up the children so Vivige can go with you."

"*Bon.* Later you and I can talk some more. What do you say we make this a memorable Christmas for the whole family? We all need a release from grief."

He watched the struggle she was having before she lifted her head and gave him a smile that masked whatever she was really thinking. "That's exactly what we need. With the weight of the whole company on your shoulders right now because of Jules's illness, it's a miracle you could take the time to fly to Colorado. You brought Christmas to Philippe. For that I'm very grateful."

But I didn't bring it to you. Is that what you're saying, Crystal? Was Raoul wrong thinking what he'd been thinking? He'd given her a lot to ponder and knew better than to help her on with her parka or ask her to stay longer.

"There's the whole holiday ahead of us," he reminded her. "Thankfully, I'm pretty much off until the New Year unless an emergency arises."

After a slight hesitation she said, "That has to be a great relief for you. I'll see you at your parents." In a jerky motion, she reached for her hat and parka. "Now, I've got to get home."

"*Bonne nuit,* Crystal."

His good-night followed her out the door. Crystal had prayed he wouldn't walk her out to the car. To her profound relief she'd gotten her wish. Whenever they were together, wherever they were—be it inside or outside—she had trouble taking a deep breath and walked around with a suffocating feeling in her chest that refused to go away.

The memory of the way he'd looked when he'd walked into the living room a little while ago wouldn't leave her alone. In the semidark interior, he'd stood near the coffee table with one hand casually resting on the back of a chair. Wearing a white sweater and dark slacks, his virility had been too potent for her.

Taking a job that would keep them in contact with each other on a daily basis was unthinkable. Even though it would mean the world to Philippe, her instinct was to get as far away as possible from Raoul.

During the short drive to her in-laws' house, she had to admit a part of her was in shock he'd actually offered her the position. He really was trying to get her interested in her career again. Was that *all* he was interested in?

She pulled up in the drive with a shudder and buried her face in her hands. She really was a walking disaster and couldn't go on like this much longer. After a few minutes she pulled herself together and let herself in the house. The place was quiet. Arlette must have already gone to bed. Tomorrow was going to be a big day with Jules coming home. It served as a reminder that he was the reason she and Philippe had come back to France in the first place.

Now that he was getting better, it was important that peace reigned in the Broussard household. She hurried up the stairs to the bedroom. Until she took Philippe back to Breckenridge, she wouldn't fight her son. Hopefully she could get Philippe to go skiing with her. She'd take all the kids. It would be fun.

Once Christmas was over, she'd find a way to convince Philippe that the world hadn't come to an end because they were going back to Breckenridge. Maybe she'd take him to a travel agency and have the agent make out two round-trip tickets for her and Philippe—to prove that she'd be bringing him back over the Easter break. If he had something tangible in hand like an airline ticket so he could plan for the future, it just might work. *It had to.*

But it would require Raoul's cooperation, too. Since he'd insisted that he'd always be there for her and Philippe, she would put him to the test. He would have to help her convince Philippe that he'd be very busy until Easter and wouldn't have the time to spend with his nephew. They would have to make him see that Christmas had been different because Jules had been ill and everyone in the family had taken time off.

Crystal got ready for bed, but she spent a restless night tossing and turning. In the morning she awakened early in order to greet Philippe when he came home to get dressed for school. At seven-thirty he arrived with Raoul.

"Mommy?"

"In the kitchen." A totally happy boy came running and hugged her.

"Did you have a fun sleepover?" The question was unnecessary, but she asked it anyway.

"Yes! Can I do it again tonight with Albert?"

"If it's all right with your uncle, but right now you need to change. Your clothes are laid out on your bed."

"Okay. I'll be right back."

Once again she was alone with Raoul, who'd dressed in one of the company's dark green parkas with its alpine logo. Every color suited him. "Would you like some coffee? I made it fresh."

"I'd like it if Philippe and I hadn't just finished breakfast." His dark blue gaze slowly appraised her in her jeans and knit top. "You're really all right about him staying at my house again tonight?"

She darted him a glance. "It's where he wants to be."

"Thank you, Crystal. Philippe's being here has made a huge change in Papa, in everyone." His eyes darkened with emotion. "Last year I didn't bother with a tree." She heard a bleak tone in his voice that was so disturbing she couldn't bear it.

Avoiding his eyes she whispered, "Last year was a painful time for everyone."

"Would it surprise you to know Crystal Broussard has made *my* Christmas by being here?"

His words started a tremor inside her.

"Bonjour, tout le monde." Crystal lifted her head in time to see Arlette walk in the kitchen with Philippe.

Raoul kissed his mother. "I'll be by for you at eleven-thirty and we'll bring Papa home."

"Hooray! Tell *Grand-père* I'll see him after school."

"Of course I will. He's living for it." Arlette gave Philippe a big hug, then helped him on with his parka and ski hat. "Have a wonderful day."

"I will. 'Bye, Mommy."

"See you later, honey."

Crystal was shaken as she watched them leave. "What can I do to help you?" she asked Arlette after they were alone. She needed physical activity to deal with the excess energy Raoul had created with that last comment.

"I thought we'd go to the *marché* and get some things Jules loves."

"Excellent idea. When we get back I'll make him some Hello Dollies. He and Philippe both love those cookies."

Arlette squeezed her arm. "Vivige was over last evening and commented that a week ago she was sick with worry and feared things were going to get worse. But the opposite has happened. Your being here has turned everything around and injected the happiness that's been missing."

"I know what you're saying. My little boy is behaving like his old self, too." That was Raoul's doing.

"Forgive me for wishing you lived here all the time?"

Her comment was too much of a reminder of what she'd be giving up by refusing to accept Raoul's fantastic offer. But she couldn't live in his sphere.

She clutched the nearest chair back. "There's nothing to forgive." Needing to get past this moment she said, "I'll just run upstairs for my coat and purse. I want to buy some flowers for Jules, too. If we get to market early enough, we'll have our pick of the ones we want."

Later in the day Jules remarked on the bouquets as Raoul had helped him in the house. Arlette insisted he go straight to his bed, where he could rest until the family congregated for dinner. While Raoul visited with his father, Crystal and Vivige stayed busy in the kitchen to help get everything ready, then Crystal picked up the children.

Jules was all choked up when they gathered around him in the salon after they'd eaten. He gave Philippe back the little *Père Noël* ornament.

"I knew he'd make you better, *Grand-père.*"

Crystal's heart melted on the spot. While they were all engrossed, she slipped out to the kitchen with Vivige to do the dishes. In time, Bernard was the one who finally broke things up because everyone needed to get to bed, including Jules.

When Raoul was ready to drive the boys to his house, Philippe hurried over to Crystal to hug her good-night. This time she'd packed clothes for him to wear to school in the morning. "Guess what? Tomorrow we're going to get our angel costumes to try on."

"How exciting!" She helped him on with his parka.

"Do you know how much I'm going to miss you? This will be two nights in a row you've slept away from me."

Suddenly Philippe whispered in her ear. "Can you sleep with us?" That was the third time he'd tried to get her to be with him and Raoul.

"I think I'd better stay here with your *grand-père* just barely home."

"Okay."

Over his shoulder she sensed a pair of dark piercing blue eyes staring at the two of them. Their intensity left her reeling. "Be good for Madame Fillou tomorrow."

"I'm always good."

She kissed his cheek and let him run to the man who'd become Philippe's *raison d'être*.

Soon the house had emptied. Crystal said goodnight to her in-laws and went up to bed, but she was haunted by her son's eagerness to get her and Raoul together. He was too young to have an agenda, so it meant that in his pure, simple way, he wanted the three of them to be together.

That spelled agony for Crystal, who couldn't find any peace. Maybe a long soak in the tub would help. Hoping to get her mind on something else if only for a little while, she started reading. But as absorbing as the mystery was, she kept remembering the way Raoul had stared at her earlier. She soon found herself reliving every moment with him and realized she'd get no reading done tonight and shut the book.

After getting out of the water, she got ready for bed and climbed under the covers. She could only hope sleep wouldn't elude her, as it had last night, but her mind had become a torture chamber of emotions she couldn't shut off.

When her phone rang, she assumed it was her mom and was glad for the distraction. But her senses whirled when she reached for her cell on the bedside table and saw Raoul's name. Uh-oh. Maybe he was having a problem with Philippe. She couldn't comprehend it, but no one knew all the things going on inside her son. She clicked on. "Raoul?"

"Sorry to bother you, Crystal, but I've been called out on an emergency and have to go. The boys are asleep. Could you come over now?"

"I'll be there as soon as I can." She shot out of bed and started getting dressed. "What's happened?"

"One of the guides took out a small party this morning for a day climb, but never returned. There's been no word from him. We know where he was headed. I'm going out with a search party, but it's anyone's guess how long I'll have to be gone."

Her hand almost crushed the cell phone she was holding. If anything happened to Raoul... "I'm heading out of the house now. See you in a minute." She hung up and got in the car.

On the short drive over she had to remind herself Raoul had been going out on emergencies for years. He was the most sought-after mountaineer in the Alps. But he wasn't infallible. Eric's horrible death during the downhill had taught her that a champion of champions was still susceptible to the dangers other mortals faced.

By the time she'd pulled up in the drive, he appeared at the side of the car and opened the door for her. Dressed in all his gear for a night climb, her heart did its own version of a tremor.

"Thanks for getting here so fast." His voice sounded an octave lower than usual. "The guest bedroom is waiting for you."

She nodded. "Please be careful."

"I'm always careful, *ma belle.*"

"Don't joke, Raoul. Not about this."

"Are you telling me you'd miss me?"

Her heart was in her throat. "You know very well how we'd all feel if you—" She couldn't say it and said instead, "If you got into trouble. It could happen."

"I'm not talking about how everyone else would feel," he growled. "I'm talking about *you.*"

Heat swept into her cheeks. "Of course I'd miss you."

"That's all I wanted to hear. Keep thinking about my offer and we'll talk about it when I'm back."

She'd already thought about it. It was more out of the question than ever.

"I don't want to be in the program if Uncle Raoul isn't going to be there."

The school Christmas performance was about to begin. Philippe had no idea the kind of agony Crystal was in right now dealing with two crises, both of them of earthshaking proportions. The thing she'd hoped would never happen, *had* happened.

No one had seen or heard from Raoul since Thursday night. Though it didn't alarm the family because dealing with emergencies was a part of his life, her son didn't understand that. As for Crystal, she was in turmoil fearing that something awful had happened to him.

It was now Saturday afternoon. She'd had a struggle getting Philippe in the car so she could drive him to school to get ready. "You have to carry on, honey. Your teacher has been so nice to let you go to class with Albert. If you were to let her down, that wouldn't be fair to her."

There was no response. "Your grandfather is coming just to see you." Still no reaction. "Do you think it would make your uncle happy to know you quit at the last minute?" Maybe that argument would help since nothing else had worked.

She was looking at him through the rearview mirror. He put his head down. "No."

"Uncle Bernard's going to be taking movies. That means your uncle Raoul will be able to watch them after he gets home."

"What if he died like Daddy?" Out of the mouth of a child. Philippe had just voiced the fear lurking in her heart ever since Raoul had phoned about the emergency. With two deaths already in the family, it wasn't hard to make the leap to a place too awful to contemplate.

"That's not going to happen," she said matter-of-factly. *Fate wouldn't be so cruel.* "It's his job to help people. He'll be back as soon as he can, so cheer up. Today's a happy day. I can't wait to see you in the Christmas program. Just think. Now that you and Albert will be out of school, you can play together all the time."

She pulled into the parking lot. With all the visitors arriving, it was filling up fast. Crystal turned off the motor. "Look—there's your grandmother's car and Uncle Bernard's! That means everyone is here. Come on. Let's hurry inside so you can get into your costume."

"I don't see Uncle Raoul's car."

"Tell you what. When we get inside your room to put on your costume, I'll phone him and see if he answers." Finally she'd said something to strike a chord because he undid his seat belt and got out of the car.

Together they walked inside the building and headed for his class. The boys' teacher had put the costumes out on the tables. Their angel outfits were white with gold trim and a gold halo. He and Albert looked adorable in them, but a certain six-year-old wasn't acting that way.

"Did you call him again?"

"Yes, but he's not answering. He will when he can."

Vivige knew what was happening and flashed her a commiserating glance as she fastened up the backs of their costumes.

"*Attention.* It's time for the parents to go to the auditorium."

At the sound of the teacher's voice, Philippe's face started to crumble. "I don't want to sing."

Crystal couldn't force him. Her son's heart was breaking for fear something had happened to Raoul. Those feelings ran deep in his psyche.

She got down on her haunches and smoothed the tears from his cheeks. "All right, honey. You don't have to be in the program. Will you at least come with me so we can watch it together?"

"Yes," he croaked.

"That's good because Fleur and Lise are going to be singing with their classes, too."

She stood up and caught Madame Fillou's eye. The teacher could see something was wrong and nodded.

Clasping his hand, Crystal started walking them behind Vivige. When her sister-in-law opened the door into the hall, Philippe's cry rang throughout the room. "Hey—you're back!" He let go of Crystal's hand and literally flew into Raoul's arms.

One of the mothers smiled at Crystal. "Your son is certainly crazy about his good-looking father. I never saw anything like it. Lucky you." She winked.

Crystal smiled back, but her emotions were in chaos. She'd never seen anything like it, either, as she watched the two of them hug. It wasn't the normal hug a nephew gave an uncle coming and going. This was her son who'd been suffering trauma since discovering his uncle had gone on a rescue mission—the uncle Philippe had known from birth and had turned to whenever Eric hadn't been there.

Through the years a bond had been forged and another truth had to be faced. All the time Eric had been a part-time father, Raoul had done the heavy-duty round-the-clock parenting. Somewhere along the way he'd become the daddy.

If Suzanne had lived and they'd had children, things would have been different. But, the reality was, Philippe had drawn close to Raoul and her little boy thrived on the love he gave him.

"Philippe, honey—your teacher wants you to get in line."

"Okay." His uncle's appearance had turned him back into a sweet angel.

Raoul put him down. "We'll be out in front watching you."

Crystal blew him a kiss, then hurried to join Vivige. They made their way into the auditorium where the rest of the family were saving seats. Crystal sat next to Jules with Vivige on her other side. Bernard had the camera ready.

Out of the corner of her eye Crystal saw Raoul sit next to his mother. Jules wore a permanent smile. For the next hour they were treated to a wonderful Christmas program. All the cousins performed beautifully, and it was as if Philippe had been in the school all year.

When they got to the part where they sang "Silent Night," the carol mocked the turmoil going on inside of Crystal. Even though Raoul had returned, the fear that something had happened to him had upset her so much, it had caused havoc with her stomach. A minute before the program was over, she turned to Vivige.

"I suddenly need a restroom. Will you see to Philippe? I'll meet you all at the house."

"You poor thing. Of course."

She rushed past the crowd and was the first one to leave the auditorium. Because she was so fast, she beat the others exiting the parking lot and raced home. Once upstairs, she thought she'd lose her lunch; but, by that time, the nausea had subsided.

Once she'd freshened up, she planned to go back downstairs and hug her son, but there was a knock on the door. Surprised Philippe didn't just burst in, she opened it and met a grim-faced Raoul in the entry. He came inside, nudging the door shut behind him with his foot.

"What happened to make you bolt like that after the program?"

"I had a hard time with Philippe before you came to his schoolroom. My stomach cramped up because of delayed stress, but I'm fine now."

"The hell you are. It's something else."

She could never hide anything from him. "No, Raoul. I—I was just so thankful you came when you did," she said, her voice faltering.

"So thankful it made you sick?"

Crystal struggled for breath. "Before you showed up, Philippe was afraid you'd died."

A ring of white appeared around his compelling mouth. "Is that what you thought, too?" When she didn't say anything because she was afraid to admit it, he held her upper arms, shaking her gently. "Tell me the truth."

"I didn't want to think it because—because I couldn't bear the thought."

"Of what?" he demanded.

"Of you being gone—" She averted her eyes. "The family couldn't handle another tragedy."

His sudden intake of breath sounded like a volcanic fissure erupting. "So it wasn't personal?" He'd brought her body right up against his.

"Raoul—" she cried in torment, but that was the only word to escape her lips before he lowered his dark head and found her mouth. Her body quivered as he closed his mouth over hers in a man's kiss so hot with desire it began melting her bones.

Crystal had already caught flame and opened up to him, giving in to her terrible hunger for him. She heard his unmistakable moan of longing before he deepened their kiss. The kind of rapture she'd never known sent out voluptuous heat, encasing them in a fire too marvelous to describe.

To be tasting and loving him like this when she'd dreamed about it for so long had her soaring. When he unexpectedly wrenched his mouth from hers, leaving her reeling, she gasped in the aftershock and took a step away from his arms.

What had she done?

"You—you shouldn't have done that, Raoul," she said, her voice shaking while she wobbled in place. The feel of him still held her in its grip.

His eyes glittered dangerously. "Hate me all you want, but you'd be lying if you told me you didn't enjoy that."

Her cheeks burned as if she had a fever. "Yes, I enjoyed it," she admitted. "No man has kissed me since Eric. I'd forgotten how pleasurable it could be."

"Kind of like the same way you forgot how much you loved to ski," he persisted. "Look what happened when you gave yourself permission to embrace life again."

Fighting for her life she said, "Yes, and that's because of the offer you made me. I've done nothing but think about it, so I might as well give you my answer now."

Raoul's body broke out in a cold sweat. This was it, the answer he'd been waiting for since the other night at his house.

He watched her brace her legs against the end of the bed, as if she needed support. "This won't take long." He could hear her rapid breathing.

"Go on," he said, moving toward her.

"I've considered it from every angle. Your offer

was so incredibly generous, I'm still overwhelmed by it."

His lungs froze. If his theory was wrong and she took him up on it, then it meant she didn't have the feelings for him he had for her.

"I happen to know it's unprecedented," she continued, "which makes what I have to tell you sound like I'm the most ungrateful wretch who ever lived. But I'm afraid I'm going to have to turn it down because I've decided to make a new life for myself and Philippe in Breckenridge."

The blood pounded in his ears.

"After we return, I'm going to start a ski school. I'm also going to buy Philippe and I a house of our own and get him enrolled in some activities like karate. At some point I'm also going to rent a piano in the hope he might take to it. Raising a well-rounded child is important to me. Though I didn't like piano lessons when I was younger, it taught me music and I think it's important."

Crystal could talk all she wanted, but Raoul was too elated to listen and didn't buy a word of it.

"I know you told me to think about it and give you my answer when I was ready. Well the truth is, I wanted to tell you 'no' when you first made the offer, but that would have seemed unconscionably rude of me."

He shifted his weight, struggling to contain emotions that were spilling out in every direction. "You don't know how to be rude, Crystal. If you don't feel that establishing a ski school here is for you, then I won't bring it up again. My concern was to be of help to you and Philippe any way I could."

"You've always been there for us. There've been times when I don't know what I...we would have done without you."

The betraying choice of words wasn't wasted on him. "I'll always be here for you. You know that."

It was fascinating to watch the way her hands rubbed against womanly hips in an unconscious gesture. The sister-in-law he'd once known had never betrayed her nervousness around him like this. He was seeing a new phenomenon she'd only started to display since he'd flown to Colorado.

"I'll never forget your offer. Thank you for all you've done for Philippe. He's the most fortunate little boy I know to have you for his uncle."

"You know how I feel about him. In fact, one of the reasons I came upstairs was to tell you I've arranged for a sleigh ride for everyone who wants to go. It's my treat to the children for putting on such a wonderful performance. See you downstairs? Be sure to dress warmly."

He purposely held himself back from touching her again because he couldn't trust himself within ten feet of her right now. After he left the room, he stopped at the stair landing to send Des a text.

She turned me down flat. Joy to the world.

CHAPTER SIX

HATE ME ALL YOU WANT, but you'd be lying if you told me you didn't enjoy that.

Crystal stood there for a long time, taking in shallow breaths while the ramifications of what he'd done began to set in. With that soul-destroying kiss he'd crossed over the line and broken all the rules. What was it Eric had once told her about his elder brother?

Raoul makes up his own rules as he goes along. That's why he's the best of the best at what he does.

He *was* the best. Seconds ago she'd turned down an offer no other champion skier in her right mind would do. Yet, all the while she'd been giving him her reasons, she'd had the feeling he wasn't listening because he knew Philippe wasn't on board with any of it.

She'd kept waiting for him to raise objections. In a way, she'd been anticipating a fight. Not the cat-and-dog kind, naturally. Raoul knew how to put up arguments couched with logic and reason that made it difficult for her to ever come out the winner. But just a little while ago when she'd been frank with him, he'd said nothing to dissuade her. By not bringing any pressure to bear, it had thrown her off balance.

With that kiss, it meant all those growing feelings

she'd tried to deny before leaving for Colorado had been visible to Raoul on some sensory level. Otherwise he wouldn't have done what he did with the kind of mastery he'd shown.

While she wrestled with what she planned to do about it for the rest of the holidays, Philippe came bursting into her room.

"Mommy? Were you sick?"

All her child needed was more worry. She hugged him hard. "I had a little tummy ache, but it's all better. Do you know you were the best angel in the whole program? I'm so proud of you."

"Thanks. Uncle Raoul said so, too. Now we've got to hurry 'cause he's taking us for a long sleigh ride!"

"I know. We need to get our parkas and boots on."

The last thing she wanted to do was face anyone, but she had to put on a happy front for Philippe. Once they'd gathered their things, they left her bedroom. On the way down she gave herself a talk about getting control of her life. She'd taken charge once before and had left Chamonix. She could do it again. It was time to act like a mother in charge of her son and do what was best for both of them.

From here on out she needed to play her role as the happy aunt to the hilt. No one would be able to see the crack in her defense put there by Raoul himself. Her brother-in-law had become her greatest adversary, but no one else knew it.

Maybe it was better he'd drawn the fragile curtain aside to expose what had been the elephant in the room for so long she couldn't bear it anymore. Now that she'd reached flash point and had given in to her desires for that brief moment, she had no choice but to set up a counterstrategy to end the conflict for good. You fought fire with fire. That's what she intended to do.

"Are you feeling all right now?"

Avoiding Raoul's shuttered gaze, Crystal turned to Arlette. "Much. I think maybe I've been eating too many pieces of marzipan, so I'm going to stay away from it."

"Oh, dear. I'm sorry."

"It's my fault for being a glutton. When I used to race, I'd eat tons of it for the calories and burn them off. But I've found I can't do that anymore. It's been sitting in my tummy like a pile of rocks."

Everyone broke into gales of laughter except Raoul. He knew the truth, but went along with her performance. That was good. She'd come down to the salon armed with a plan that was now set in stone.

Everyone hugged the grandparents goodbye and left the house in two cars. Crystal got in the front seat of Raoul's car. The boys climbed in back.

"Where are we going, Uncle Raoul?"

"To the same farm where I took you before, Albert."

"Did you bring the sleigh bells?" Philippe cried out excitely.

"I did. They're in the back of my car."

"Goody!"

The boys waved to the girls riding in Bernard's car. Before long they reached the farm on one of the lower hillsides. A large sleigh and a small one, each with two horses, sat waiting for them along the snow packed lane. Their drivers, two older Savoyards, waved to them. With an overcast sky and the Alps in the background, the whole alpine winter scene didn't look quite real and could have graced a Christmas card.

"Can Albert and I go in the small sleigh?"

"Maybe another time, Philippe. I need a chance to talk to your mother, and this would be a good time to do it."

Crystal shivered. She couldn't imagine they had anything to talk about now. But remembering her plan to fight fire with fire, she didn't try to accommodate her son's wishes.

"Okay." To her shock, he went along with it. Except for when Raoul had to be gone on that emergency, her son had changed a lot and was so much more settled down, she hardly knew him.

Raoul pulled to a stop at the side of the road and got out. With Bernard's help they attached the bells to the horses' trappings on the big sleigh, delighting the boys. The children climbed in with Vivige and Bernard, divvying up blankets for everyone who sat where they wanted.

"Hi, Mommy!" Philippe waved to her. She waved back, but her attention was drawn to Raoul, who walked back to the smaller sleigh where she was sitting. His dark hair was partially covered by his navy ski hat. With the bite of the air, his warm complexion brought out his striking features. He was so alive and heartbreakingly handsome, it hurt to look at him.

She quickly focused on their moustached driver in his old mountain hat who turned around to make sure they were settled. Then he shook the reins. Once the horses received that signal, they moved forward behind the other sleigh. She could hear the children whooping it up in the distance.

As the horses paced along in rhythm, the sleigh bells made their distinctive sounds while the sleigh swished and glided across the snow. The outing was one of sheer enchantment, carrying her back to the other magical morning on the ski slopes with Raoul.

The scene right now was too surreal for Crystal. She closed her eyes for a little while and just listened while she dreamed about what it would be like if he had any deeper feelings for her.

Finally, today, the kiss of a lover full of hot-blooded passion had brought her own feelings closer to the surface to be acknowledged. But Raoul wasn't her lover. He was a man who'd been with other women since Suzanne and enjoyed them. She knew he did, especially when he'd gone on climbing trips with Des.

The kiss he'd given her in the bedroom was something he'd done in the nature of an experiment in order to wake her up to the possibilities of life, but it hadn't been prompted by the earthshaking desire she had for him. When she'd told him she couldn't accept his offer to run a ski school here, he'd left it alone. His calm acceptance gave her the proof he could compartmentalize his feelings for the good of the moment.

To belong to him was a pipe dream on her part. Just entertaining the thought terrified her because she had to remember that the only person who truly mattered was Philippe.

Even if Raoul did feel something for her, if the world were to hear they were a couple, the press would make it into a scandal that would follow her son for the rest of his life. There'd be questions as to whether Philippe was the son of France's great sporting hero, or the son of Raoul Broussard—Eric's brother and a celebrity in his own right among the mountaineers of Europe.

She couldn't do that to her precious boy. He was an innocent child who didn't deserve to grow up under an ugly cloud of vicious lies and rumors.

No…it was a dream she had to bury. The big question now was how to rein in her emotions until she left France with her son.

"You're so immersed in thought, I was afraid you'd forgotten I was here." His deep voice insinuated itself inside her skin.

Raoul, Raoul.

Her eyes opened to a sky that had deepened into darkness. He'd leaned closer to her, bringing the familiar male scent she loved. Their breath curled in the night air and mingled. "To be honest, I was enjoying the silence. It's heavenly out here, like we're being pulled across a fantastic moonscape."

"You sound happy. Shades of the old Crystal are coming out in you more and more."

"The *old* Crystal?" she questioned in surprise.

"*Oui, ma belle.* The first time I met you, you were this happy, sunny girl whose spirit pervaded our entire household. But slowly I saw a difference come over you and we both know why. Eric or no Eric, Philippe is the luckiest boy in the world to have a mother like you."

That's what he'd brought Crystal out here to tell her? He wanted to compliment her for being a good mom? He didn't want to…

Crystal had to stop what she was thinking. "Thank you," she said in a shaky whisper.

"He's inherited your naturally sunny disposition. When he's around, he's like a breath of fresh air."

His emotion when he talked about her son shook her to the depths. There was a sudden tension-filled silence brought on because she didn't know what to say and shouldn't have come on this sleigh ride with him.

"As long as you were so honest with me at Chez Pierre the other day," he continued, "there's something I should have told you while we were talking. It's something I should have told the whole family after Suzanne died."

Her body went taut. She was almost afraid to hear what he was about to tell her. Her gaze shot to his. She noticed a nerve throbbing at the corner of his mouth. "What is it?"

"When the results of the autopsy came through, it was confirmed she was pregnant, but neither of us knew it at the time."

Crystal tried to smother her horrified gasp.

"For a long time I was angry at the world for such a senseless tragedy," he rasped. "But mostly I couldn't forgive myself for not being with her when she needed me. I wasn't able to save her. *Me*—the great mountaineer!"

"Raoul—" she cried in anguish for him and grasped his hand. He and Suzanne were going to have a baby.... Crystal knew all about guilt and suffered fresh pain for him. "No wonder you shut off your feelings for such a long time."

"I'm afraid I did more than that!" His eyes flashed. "I resented Eric for his cavalier treatment of you. Here he had a wife and son, and he didn't value either of you the way he should have."

Crystal had no idea all this had gone on inside over the last few years.

"When he died, I was in even more despair over the guilt I felt for having judged him when it wasn't my place."

"You don't need to tell me about guilt," she murmured.

"There's more," he groaned out. "There were even times when I resented *you*."

She swallowed hard. "Why?"

"Because you had your son and it was a reminder to me of everything I'd lost. Perhaps now you understand why Philippe is doubly precious to me."

She nodded. Oh, yes.

It explained why he'd sounded accusatory when he'd first arrived in Breckenridge. She now understood why the monthly phone calls from Raoul had been so terse and unsatisfactory over the last year. He'd kept their conversations short before asking to speak to Philippe.

She'd been hurt by his manner and feared more of the same if she decided to phone him. So she hadn't done it, but it had cost her son so much unhappiness.

Besides losing his wife, Raoul had lost his unborn child. Philippe had lost his father. On some deeper lever the two of them had sensed each other's loss and had reached out for comfort. The bond between them ran fathoms deep.

Raoul's confession had cleared up so many questions, she realized.

"I'm sorry for being so hard on you, Crystal," he said against the tips of her fingers before kissing them.

"You think I don't understand?"

He raised his head. His eyes were dark blue pools of light. "That's the point. I know you do, and I'm humbled by it." This time when he kissed her lips, it was a kiss of gratitude that couldn't be mistaken for anything else. It explained his other kiss with all its pent-up frustration and pain.

Oh, yes, she understood it all.

When he quickly relinquished her mouth, she realized the sleigh had stopped. She looked around. All she could see was Raoul's car. "I didn't realize we were back. The others have already gone home."

A quiet smile broke out on his handsome face. "We're due at Vivige's for a party."

"I didn't know that."

"This is *their* surprise for the children. A celebration slumber party. Let's go, shall we?"

In a few minutes they'd driven to the cousins' roomy chalet for hot chocolate and Vivige's special Christmas plum cake.

Philippe was so happy he looked like he would burst. "I wish we could take a sleigh ride every day. Don't you, Mommy?"

She kissed his frozen cheeks, avoiding Raoul's gaze that seemed to follow her everywhere she turned. "It was wonderful, but if we did it every day, it wouldn't seem so special."

"Come on, Philippe," Albert called to him. "We're going to play table tennis. Papa says it's the men against the women."

"Goody!"

Their playroom on the second floor was a child's dream. Bernard had everything set up. "Albert? You'll play against Lise. Philippe against Fleur. I'll beat your mother." Everyone laughed hard. "Raoul against Crystal. Then we'll rotate partners three more times. May the best men win."

"Papa—" the girls cried out in protest before giggling.

For the next hour it was a battle to the death with more wins for the men of the house.

"I don't think it's fair," Fleur pouted.

Crystal gave her a big hug. "It isn't." She bent down and whispered, "Where's your game of Escargot? We'll show up the men."

Her face lit up. "It's right there on the shelf." She ran to get it.

It was kind of like the game of hopscotch, requiring lots of hopping to get to the center of a large snail, with lots of contortions and accidents as spaces were claimed and initialed by each player so you couldn't step on them without receiving a penalty.

As it turned out, their uncle Raoul lost the competition for the men when he tried to do the impossible and landed in the middle of the game on his back. It sent the girls into squeals of laughter and pretty soon everyone joined in.

Crystal was still laughing hard when her eyes accidentally met Raoul's as he got to his feet. The look he shot her sent a private message that bespoke pleasure. They'd shared so much over the last few days, she'd felt a change in their relationship. As if they were friends like they'd been when Suzanne was alive, and yet it felt so different now.

Reaching for Philippe, she pulled him aside. "It's late and I need to get back to your grandparents in case they need me for any reason. Give me a kiss good-night and I'll see you in the morning."

"Good night, Mommy." He hugged and kissed her hard. This was her happy child, the one she never wanted to see disappear again.

She made the rounds hugging the children, then thanked Vivige and Bernard for a wonderful time. "I'll pick the children up tomorrow and take them skiing."

Philippe darted over to her and whispered in her ear. "You're going to take us skiing?"

"Yes," she whispered back.

"But I thought you didn't like to ski anymore."

"I love it, honey."

His eyes rounded. "So do I!"

"You do? I thought maybe you didn't like it because you didn't want to go with Grandpa."

He stared at her with those innocent blue eyes. "I wanted *you* to take me."

"Oh, darling." She clutched him to her. So many misunderstandings. Over her shoulder she saw Raoul watching them and wondered if his eyes were glistening, or maybe it was a trick of the light.

After letting him go, she left the house and walked out to Raoul's car. He was only a few steps behind her. Soon they were on their way back to Les Pecles. With Christmas so close, the decorated streets were filled with locals and tourists enjoying an atmosphere like nowhere else in the world.

Today there'd been moments when she'd experienced every emotion—from fear, to sadness, to excitement and incomparable joy that Raoul had returned safely from his rescue expedition. He was the reason for all of those feelings. For hours she'd had a legitimate excuse to be in his company. There was no one like him and never would be.

When they reached the house, Jules and Arlette were still up. While Raoul stored the sleigh bells, she told them about the sleigh ride and the party at Vivige's house.

Her father-in-law sat there with tears in his eyes. "You've got that smile back."

"It was a perfect day, Jules. You look wonderful. Are you really feeling better?"

"Mais oui, ma fille."

Arlette smiled at her. "He's looking more like his old self every day. It's because we have our whole family around us. We've been talking about having a family picture professionally done after Christmas right here by the tree. What do you think?"

"It will make a wonderful souvenir for Philippe."

"Who's talking souvenirs?" Raoul had just entered the salon. His eyes impaled her. "You just got here." Though he'd said it in a light tone, she knew it had upset him. Now she understood why. He would miss Philippe horribly when they left.

His father chuckled. "Come in and sit, *mon fils.* That is, if you can. Crystal told us about your accident."

To her surprise a low chuckle came out of Raoul, changing his mood. She felt it resonate to her insides. "It was Crystal's fault. She put Fleur up to getting out that blasted game."

Jules hooted. "It's a good thing your clients didn't see it happen or they'd take their business elsewhere."

"I think it was worth it. Don't you, Crystal?" That question said in his deep male voice haunted her. His eyes forced her to look at him. "Have you ever seen Philippe have more fun?"

She knew what he was really asking. "Thanks to you, I think today topped everything in his world." *And mine.*

Though he still smiled, she got the feeling her answer didn't seem to please him.

His father looked at him. "Was anyone injured in that climbing party you rescued?"

"Two of them got hypothermia, but they're doing fine now."

"What happened?"

"One of the climbers didn't throw his ax hard enough. The ice didn't hold and he fell. It took the guide time to get down to him on the ropes. By then it was dark and they decided to wait it out until daylight."

"What chute was it?"

"The *'épingle.'*"

His father nodded. "That's too difficult a place for inexperienced climbers."

"I agree and told the guide."

"Well, all's well that ends well. I'm glad you got back safely. I think I'm ready for bed now. Coming, Arlette?" She nodded. Everyone got to their feet.

"I'll lock up the house for you, *Papa.*"

"Merci, mon fils."

They all kissed good-night, leaving Raoul alone with Crystal. After they'd gone upstairs, she turned to him. "Thank you for the sleigh ride. I think you know it was like a day out of time, one that neither Philippe or I will ever forget." Her voice throbbed.

"You keep giving goodbye speeches. Can't you let it rest until you leave?"

"It was a figure of speech, but as you and I both know, nothing's forever."

That forbidding look stole over his face once more. It had been missing for the last two days. "Wouldn't it be horrifying if it were true," he muttered, absently rubbing his chest. "I'll come by tomorrow with ski gear for you and Philippe from the shop. With four children, we'll need two cars."

Her pulse accelerated to a wild pitch. She'd hoped he'd want to join them. "They'll love it more if you're there." The children would provide a buffer so she could enjoy his company. A stab of pain jolted her to realize the New Year would be here before she knew it. The thought of being without Raoul was anathema to her now.

"Before you go, I have a question. I know what Lise and Fleur want for Christmas, but I need help with Albert. What do you think?"

"He loves games with plastic pieces and can never have enough."

"That helps me. In town I saw a pirate ship he could build. I don't think he has one. At least I didn't see one over there this evening."

"I'm pretty sure he doesn't. He and Philippe will have a lot of fun putting it together."

She nodded. "See you tomorrow."

"*Bonne nuit,* Crystal."

CHAPTER SEVEN

ALBERT RAN UP TO Raoul, who was putting all their ski equipment in the car. "Now that we're through skiing, will you take us to that Christmas movie?" Philippe was right behind him. "Please?"

Raoul's gaze flicked to Crystal's. She'd just handed him Fleur's skis and poles. "What do you think?"

"I'd like to see it myself."

"Hooray," the children shouted. The girls got in Crystal's car. Albert and Philippe had already claimed Raoul's.

Satisfied that Crystal wasn't trying to get away from him, Raoul's body relaxed. After he'd closed the trunk she said, "With Christmas Eve tomorrow, I'm sure Arlette and Vivige are appreciating the free time to get a lot of things done today. I'll follow you to the complex."

They drove in tandem from the beginners' slopes at Argentière to the center of Chamonix, where they had lunch, then walked to the movie theater. Raoul had been loving this too much. It gutted him to think of it ending.

When they went inside, the kids chose to sit together. Raoul and Crystal sat a couple of rows behind them. The place was packed. There was so much noise, no one would hear if they whispered.

He handed her some candy but she refused. "We got here just in time."

"I know. It's perfect. I can tell my son feels very grown up being here without his mother sitting at his side like he's a baby."

Raoul glanced at her lovely profile. "Being with his cousins has given him a lot more confidence."

"I'm going to have to work on some more play dates for him when we're back in Colorado."

His stomach knotted to even hear the word. He hated to tell her this, but if she thought she'd had problems with him over the last year, it was going to be much harder for him to go back now. But instead of getting into it with her on such a fabulous day, he changed the subject.

"I don't know about you, but I think Lise is turning into an excellent skier."

"You know why. She's fearless. Provided she starts working on her technique, there might be another medalist in the family one day."

"Just like you."

She turned her head to glance at him. "Like you, too. Des once told me you're so amazing when you scale those sheer walls, even he finds himself swallowing hard."

"He told you that to keep your attention. In case you didn't know it, he had a crush on you."

"Now you're being ridiculous."

"Not at all. He bemoaned the fact that he couldn't find a woman like you."

"Like me?"

"Um. The kind a man's dreams are made of." Raoul could have sworn she blushed.

"I had no idea."

"That's a quality I admire about you. You're very *un*self-aware."

"Are you chatting me up?" she teased unexpectedly.

A chuckle escaped his throat. "Is it working?"

"Chut!" someone said from behind them.

Crystal flashed Raoul an embarrassed look and sank a little lower in her seat. In her vulnerability he'd never wanted to kiss her more than at this moment, but there wasn't anything he could do about it. He decided it was just as well because this wasn't the place to do what he really wanted to do with her.

He had no clue what the movie was about, not while his body ached with longings that needed assuaging soon. It was an actual physical relief when the film ended and they could get out in the cold air, where he could walk off the energy created by simply sitting next to her.

They drove back to Vivige's for soup and fruit. Then Crystal excused her and Philippe. She'd promised to help his mother with some cooking before going to bed.

He followed them home to see how his father was faring. Along with Philippe, the three of them played some board games. Total entertainment. The last thing Raoul wanted to do was go back to his empty house. Every so often he went into the kitchen for a snack. Crystal smiled at him while she was working. "Who's winning?"

"Philippe."

"Again? Isn't that about the tenth time?"

"I took a leaf out of your book from the other day."

Her broad smile caught at his heart. "You're spoiling him."

"That's what I'm here for." When she turned her head away too quickly, he realized he needed to leave. "I'll see you tomorrow." He started out of the kitchen.

"Thank you for another wonderful day, Raoul," she called over his shoulder. He kept going before he lost control completely and dragged her off to some secluded place.

Christmas Eve Day meant Vivige and Arlette were busy getting everything ready for the night's festivities. Crystal had already volunteered to take the children to do their own Christmas shopping.

First she took them to lunch downtown. While they were eating, Philippe told her what he wanted to buy Raoul.

"A hat? Really? What kind?"

He looked up at her with excitement. "One like those farmers who took us on the sleigh ride the other night. I told our driver I liked his hat and Uncle Raoul said he did, too."

"Oh…you mean an alpine hat." No one would look more dashing in one than Raoul. Her heart thumped so hard, it almost knocked her over. "You really think Raoul would like one of those?"

"I know he would 'cause he told me nobody ever gave him one and he always wished he had one just like it." Come to think of it, she'd never seen Raoul in anything but a ski hat.

"Well then, that settles it."

After they ate she said, "Let's go in that shop across the street and you can pick out the one you want."

The children were just as excited as Philippe because there were all kinds of hats and alpine pins and scarves. While one shop clerk helped them look for something special to buy their father, Philippe spoke to the other salesman and described what he wanted.

"You mean a Savoyard style hat. Green or gray?"

"Green! He wears a green coat at the alpine club."

"Ah. He's a mountain climber."

"Yup. He owns it."

Crystal couldn't help but chuckle. Philippe was so proud of him.

The salesman winked at her. "Are we talking about Raoul Broussard?"

"Yes. He's my uncle!"

"You have a very famous uncle, and the green is the perfect choice. But instead of this feather, let's put an ice-ax pin on the side of the braid along with a little pin of the French flag and the other flag of Chamonix. I'll show you." As soon as he'd fixed everything, he handed it to Philippe. "What do you think?"

Her son's eyes shone with delight. "I love it!"

"We'll take it," Crystal murmured. "Do you gift-wrap?"

He nodded.

She looked at Philippe. "Why don't you run over to see what Albert is getting while I pay for this."

"Okay."

She pulled out her credit card. The second he took off to join the others, she turned to the salesman. "Do you have smaller hats for children?"

"They're in the children's department."

"Could you find out if there's one like this and have it sent over?"

"Of course."

"Wonderful."

"Do you have a little pin with the American flag?"

"Yes. Right over here."

"Then will you pin it in the smaller hat along with another ice ax and flag of Chamonix? I want this to be a surprise."

He smiled. "I'd be happy to. This'll take a few minutes."

She walked over to the children, who'd decided on their purchases. She paid the other clerk for them, then gathered her gifts and they left the shop for her car.

Philippe was so excited, he was like a top spinning out of control. "What are we going to do now?"

"It's almost six o'clock. We're going to go to both our houses so everyone can have a nap." Her announcement was met with cries of disappointment. "You have to sleep, otherwise you won't be able to stay awake for Christmas Mass and dinner afterward. Remember?"

Everyone would be sleeping at the grandparents' house and open their presents in the morning. Knowing they would all be together helped Philippe not to fight her on it.

"Okay, but I'm not tired."

She reached out to tousle her son's blond head. "You will be. I'll lie down with you. I bet we both fall sound asleep." It wouldn't surprise her if she did. After the incredible day with Raoul yesterday, she was in so much pain at the idea of leaving him, she'd cried part of the night and didn't really sleep that much.

As she dropped Vivige's children off at their house

with their purchases, Philippe turned to Albert. "Uncle Raoul said to be sure and pick out your biggest pair of shoes to put in front of *Grand-mère's* fireplace tonight."

"Yeah." Albert grinned. "We get more candy that way."

"See you later," he called after them.

After she drove them home, she passed through the kitchen to hide her gift for Philippe in a cupboard where he wouldn't think to look. Jules watched her while he helped Arlette make her famous Matafan, a Savoyard tradition at their house. They were a kind of light and fluffy pancake piled one on top of the other, a little like a soufflé. But they didn't deflate and would be the scrumptious traditional Christmas snack before they went to church.

"Those look wonderful, Arlette."

"I think they're turning out all right. Did you have a good time?"

"The best. Those children are darling and so good together."

Jules smiled at her. "Where's *mon petit-fils?*"

"He's hiding his present for Raoul. Then we're going to take a long nap before we leave for the *Messe de Minuit.*"

His blue eyes twinkled. "That's exactly what we're going to do when we've finished here. Raoul will come by for us at eleven."

"That time is going to be here before we know it." Crystal gave them both a kiss on the cheek to hide the fluttery sensation in the pit of her stomach.

After Arlette kissed her back she said, "Are you all right, Crystal? You feel a little warm to me."

Oh, no. "It's too much excitement. I'm worse than the children," she explained before rushing out of the kitchen. After last night she couldn't imagine how she was going to get through tonight and pretend everything was normal.

Last night before he'd left the kitchen, she'd almost thrown herself into his arms and begged him to carry her upstairs, where they could lose themselves in each other. Thank heaven she'd held back. It was a dream, not a reality. But it didn't ease her burning desire for him, and now it seemed she was literally running a temperature.

Once upstairs, she hurried past Philippe and ran into the bathroom to take a couple of painkillers. When she came out she discovered her son studying a picture of his daddy on the winner's podium. The moment grabbed at her like a giant hand.

"You and Daddy loved to ski, huh, Mommy."

"Yes. It's how we met." She sank down on the side of the bed. He so rarely talked about Eric. It seemed she'd been waiting forever for this talk. "He was the greatest skier I've ever seen."

Philippe let out a little sigh. "I like to ski, but I don't think I could be a good skier like him. Do you think it would make Daddy mad if I learned to mountain climb?" He'd put the picture back on the bedside table.

"Oh, darling." She crushed him to her and rocked him in her arms. "No, he wouldn't be mad. He'd be the first person to tell you to do whatever you wanted. Did you know your *grand-père* was a great mountain climber in his day?"

"Yup. He and Uncle Raoul were talking about it last night while we were playing games."

"Let me ask you something, honey. Do you think Jules was disappointed because your daddy wanted to ski instead?"

He thought about it for a minute. "No."

"There. You see? He loved your father whatever he did and was so proud that he became a great skier. But if your daddy hadn't liked any sports, he still would have loved him just the same. The important thing is to be happy with yourself and what you want to do in life."

His eyes brightened. Whatever she'd just said seemed to settle a very serious problem for him. "I already know what I'm going to be."

"You do?" Inside she already knew the answer and didn't have to wait long.

"Yes. I'm going to climb mountains and be a guide like Uncle Raoul. He says when I'm older, he'll take me up on Mont Blanc. The one with the frozen crown on its head."

"I'm glad that day is still far away. Come here, sweetheart." She pulled him on the bed with her and drew the covers over them. "Let me snuggle you for a little while. I love my big boy and need some hugs."

She needed to go to church tonight. She needed help.

When next Crystal became aware of her surroundings, she found herself alone on the bed. She checked her watch. It was quarter to eleven. She couldn't believe it. Quickly, she got up from the bed and showered before doing her makeup and brushing her hair. When she was ready, she put on her navy blue three-piece wool suit. On the lapel she fastened a Christmas corsage.

As she left her room and started for the stairs,

she could hear voices below. Vivige's family had arrived. She didn't know how long they'd been here, but Philippe must have scooted out of bed and gone down to play with them. Unfortunately, he needed to get into his suit and tie. But when she spotted him in the salon, she saw that he'd already put it on and looked like a little man in it.

"Mommy!" The second he saw her, he ran over to her, his mouth full of his pancake snack. He handed her one. "I'm all ready."

"Well, you certainly are. Did *Grand-mère* help you?"

"No. Uncle Raoul came upstairs and helped me pick out my clothes." He kept on munching while Crystal's heart practically went into fibrillation.

"You were sleeping so soundly, we didn't have the heart to wake you up." Raoul had suddenly appeared out of nowhere. He, too, was eating. "I hope you don't mind."

"Of course not." Why would she care if Raoul had come into her room while she was out for the count? Even if she'd been dressed in the jeans and top she'd worn shopping, who knew in what state he'd found her? But she shouldn't have been surprised.

Raoul turned to everyone. "Now that we're all here, shall we go?"

"Can I ride with Philippe?" Albert wanted to know.

"Not this time," Bernard said. "Raoul's taking your grandparents in his car. But we'll all be together after we reach the church."

CHAPTER EIGHT

The Place du Triangle was crowded with families wanting to attend Mass. Raoul went ahead with Philippe inside the front doors of Saint-Michel church. Bernard and his family entered behind them. Crystal and the grandparents followed.

Music from the choir singing Christmas carols filled the interior, which was illuminated with candles. Raoul found them a row of seats and they all took their places. Crystal sat on the opposite end. Just once, she leaned forward and glanced down the row to see how Philippe was doing.

Her throat almost closed up from emotion to watch her son seated next to his uncle, their heads close together talking with solemn expressions. They were both so handsome, her heart was ready to burst out of its cavity.

While the Mass took place, she offered up her own prayer that Philippe would be able to handle it when the time came for him to go back to Colorado with her. So deep was her reverie, she didn't realize Jules had been staring at her.

"Nothing should be wrong on this night of all nights," he whispered. "How can I help?"

"Oh, Jules—" She'd been all right until he'd spoken to her. "You already do by just being you."

He patted her hand, but she knew he sensed something traumatic was going on inside her. In that regard he was a lot like Raoul. Both men had intuitive natures that made them the best at their jobs on the mountain and impossible to fool.

Once the service was over, they filed out quietly, but Crystal could tell the children were exploding inside with excitement because the magic hour had come. The bells pealed forth, filling Chamonix valley with their heavenly sounds.

As she reached the car, Raoul opened the rear door for his parents and Philippe. When she would have opened the front door, he took over and helped her in the car.

"It's Christmas, huh, Mommy!"

"You bet it is. Now the fun's about to begin."

"Goody!"

His happy cry made his grandparents laugh. Crystal would give everything she possessed to feel happy tonight, but no power on earth could change the fact that Raoul would always be forbidden to her. It hit her again in church. If Jules knew how she felt about his first-born son, it would be the coup de grace for the Broussard family, who'd had enough sorrow to last them a lifetime.

Before long they arrived at the house and within a few minutes, they sat down in the dining room. A beautiful creche served for the centerpiece. Their fabulous feast began with *foie gras en brioche.* Arlette had outdone herself. Soon came the salmon, capons, turkey, *boudin,* cinnamon ice cream and *bûche de Noël.*

Jules lifted his glass of wine. "This is a night to remember because all our living family is here together. Let us be thankful."

All our *living* family.

The wine rippled in Crystal's glass as she raised it with a trembling hand. She didn't dare look at Raoul.

"Can we open presents now?" Philippe asked, breaking the silence.

Arlette put her arm around his shoulders. "First we'll go in the salon and light the candles to welcome this beautiful day."

"Oh." Crystal's son had forgotten that tradition.

As the children scrambled out of the dining room, Crystal watched Bernard grab his wife under the mistletoe hanging in the doorway and kiss her soundly on the mouth.

She turned her eyes away and headed for the kitchen, where she'd left Philippe's present in the cupboard. On her way back with the sack clutched in her hand, she came up against a solid chest standing in the doorway to the dining room.

"Oh, Raoul—sorry. I—I didn't see you standing there." He didn't move so she could get past him. She felt his gaze on her mouth.

"Joyeux Noël."

The blood pounded in her ears. "Merry Christmas," she whispered back and tried to move past him, but he pulled her into his arms.

"Don't worry. Everyone's in the other room and I'm not about to let this mistletoe go to waste. Not after getting a taste of you the other night."

In the next breath he lowered his head and kissed her with a hunger that if anyone had seen them, they'd be shocked speechless. In that one, perfect moment, Crystal finally admitted the truth to herself. Over the last year, a woman's love for this remarkable man had been born in her, building inexorably bit by bit, even when she'd been asleep. She could no longer hide from the fact that she was madly, desperately in love with Raoul.

"You don't play fair," she gasped when he finally let her up for air.

The satisfied gleam in his eyes sent another dart of fear through her because she was so susceptible to him. "I'm glad you understand that." He finally removed his hands so she could hurry through to the other part of the house. Her face was so hot, she had to hope Arlette would assume she was still feverish.

The children were gathered around the tree. Acting as if nothing had happened, Raoul reached for a long match and moved next to the tree. After lighting it, he set fire to the wicks of the real candles in their little holders. When he got to the lower branches, he told each child to come up and light one.

Philippe took the last turn and very carefully lit his. She noticed his tongue stick out, which meant he was concentrating with all his might not to make a mistake. Crystal fell in love with her son all over again just watching him.

After Raoul snuffed out the match, Arlette smiled at the children. "You'll each open one present, then we'll go to bed and see what *Père Noël* has brought you in the morning. Come closer so you can pick out your names."

Thankfully, everyone was getting ready to open presents and didn't seem to notice Crystal's hot face.

She hurried over to a chair near Philippe, who was on the floor with the other children. He lifted his head when he saw her, but he looked upset. "I don't see a present with my name on it."

"I have one right here." She pulled the wrapped gift out of the sack and placed it under the tree. In an instant his face was wreathed in a smile. "Now wait until *Grand-père* tells you it's your turn," she whispered.

He nodded.

Out of the corner of her eye she saw Raoul sit down next to his parents. When she was still having palpitations, she didn't know how he could look so calm after kissing her senseless.

Jules looked around. "The first person to open a present has a first name that starts with the sixth letter of the alphabet."

Despite what Raoul had just done to Crystal, she chuckled. Trust her father-in-law to make everyone's brain have to work. It added to the excitement of course and she loved him for it.

"That's me!" Fleur jumped up and reached for her present. Everyone watched as she opened it and found a new pair of ice skates, which apparently she'd wanted.

Jules began again. "This person's name starts with the first letter of the alphabet."

"That's you, *Grand-mère*!" Fleur said.

"And Albert!" Philippe cried out, always watching out for his cousin.

"So it is." Arlette got to her feet. "Come on, Albert. Let's find our presents."

The two of them hunted around. Albert found his first. It was a new soccer ball he'd been begging for.

Arlette took a little longer to find her small package.

"Oh—these pearls are beautiful!" She turned around with tears in her eyes and hugged Jules.

He smiled, then continued. "This person's first name starts with the twelfth letter of the alphabet."

Lise popped up at once and opened her gift. She was their reader and had been given a new series of books, which appeared to delight her.

"The next name starts with the eighteenth letter."

Philippe had already done his counting and flashed Crystal a secret smile.

Having a legitimate reason to feast her eyes on Raoul, she watched his hard-muscled body get up and reach for his gift. When she looked at her son, she could tell he was dying to see his uncle's reaction.

He pulled his gift out of the box and examined it before looking around the salon. "Now who knew that I always wanted a hat exactly like this?" A giggle came out of Philippe. "Ah-ha! I thought so." Raoul put it on his dark head at a jaunty angle. The man was gorgeous.

"Do you like those little pins?" Philippe asked. "I got you an ice ax."

"I love it all!" He walked over to his nephew and picked him up to hug him hard.

Bernard grinned at him. "Now you look like the owner of the club."

"You should wear it all the time," Vivige added. "It suits you."

"It really does, *mon fils,*" Arlette chimed in.

Jules smiled at his son, telling everyone what he thought. When Raoul sat down again his father said, "The next name starts with the twenty-second letter."

"Oh—that's me!" Vivige reached for her box, but when she lifted the lid, a blush swept over her and she closed it again. Bernard pulled her down and gave her a kiss.

"I think this next gift is for someone whose name starts with the sixteenth let—" But before Jules could finish, Philippe cheered and reached for his present. Crystal held her breath until he'd opened his box and found the hat.

"Hey—" He turned to Crystal. "This is just like Uncle Raoul's! I love it!" He gave her a kiss, then ran over to his uncle. "See? We're twins!" He put it on his head.

Raoul adjusted it at the same angle as he'd done his own. "You look *sensationnel, mon gars.*" She saw him finger the little enamel American flag before he pulled Philippe onto his lap, where they watched the rest of the gift-giving together.

Jules and Bernard both received colorful wool scarves. Crystal was given a bracelet with enamelware charms of Chamonix. She knew Arlette had picked it out because Crystal had remarked on it while they'd been shopping.

With all the presents opened, Jules reached for the family Bible and read the story of Christ's birth, then he closed it. "We've all been very blessed. Now it's time to go up to bed so *Père Noël* will come."

The children made excited sounds as they gathered up their gifts. Once they'd kissed their grandparents good-night, they raced upstairs, eager to go to sleep right now because that meant presents in the morning.

Crystal and Vivige hurried into the kitchen to get the dishes done. Bernard and Raoul joined them and they made quick work of it. Before Raoul could waylay her, she dashed out of the kitchen and up to the bedroom. Thankfully Philippe was already asleep.

Tears moistened her cheeks when she saw that he'd put his hat next to his pillow. After giving him a kiss, she raised up and discovered Raoul had come into the bedroom. She almost fainted.

"Finally we can be alone." He reached for her hand. "We're going to my house."

"No, Raoul."

"Don't fight me on it, Crystal. After the way you kissed me under the mistletoe, this moment was inevitable and you know it. I can read your mind. You're terrified that once you go out the door with me, things will never go back to the way they were before."

"Please don't do this."

"I have to because the way things are right now is impossible. Something has to be done because our situation has reached the breaking point. We have too much to say to each other, so let's not waste any more time."

He pulled her with him, grabbing her coat with his other hand. On the way out of the room he turned off the lights and led her down the stairway to the front door.

"I'm afraid to go with you."

"That's honest. It's a start."

He held up the coat for her to put on, but had to fight not to grasp her shoulders and pull her back against him. A wrong move now would only increase her fear. This thing had to be done right.

With the greatest of reluctance he let his hands fall away and opened the front door for her. "You won't need your purse. When I bring you back, I'll let you in."

Raoul helped her to his car, then went around to his side and got behind the wheel.

After being sentenced to an endless twelve-month period of physical and emotional distance, it was finally over. Wherever they went from here, the past was behind them and she knew it.

Those tight bands that had constricted his lungs after he'd watched her jet climb in the air taking her and Philippe away from him, seemed to fall away. As they drove toward his house, he felt like he was taking his first deep breath of fresh air. He refused to experience that desolation ever again.

Even though she was not touching him, he felt her shiver and knew the real reason for it. "An arctic front has moved in since the sun went down. We're in for a cold freeze. When we get home I'll start a fire."

"Thank you, but I don't plan to be there long enough for you to go to the trouble."

He gave her a covert glance, noticing how she held herself taut. "That's the kind of comment the old Crystal would have made. But you heard the clock in the square strike twelve times as we left the church. When we stepped outside, something magical happened and we walked into New Year's Day. All the ghosts of Christmas past are gone."

A low moan came out of her.

"The new slate before us is as white and untouched as the snowfields our sleigh crossed over the other night. Whatever mark we make on it first, it's going to be together."

Crystal heard Raoul's vow spoken in a tone of

refined savagery that set off a burst of adrenaline. By the time they reached his house she was like a rocket ready to go off. While he got the kindling going to build a fire, she volunteered to make them coffee. Anything to keep her hands and body busy in order to retain some semblance of outer calm.

What a joke. When she took their mugs into the living room, she put them down on the table with a jerk, spilling a little. While he was adding logs to the flames, she had to run back to the kitchen for some napkins.

After she returned and mopped up the small spill, she lifted her head and found Raoul staring at her with an intensity she'd never felt before. His features had taken on a chiseled cast and his chest rose and fell with visible force. The banked fires she'd glimpsed in his eyes over the last few days were openly ablaze, sending a weakness through her body.

"I'm in love with you, Crystal."

A gasped escaped her throat. *Just like that* he'd said the words.

She staggered back to the couch, having been afraid she might never hear them, and now terrified that she had. This was why she hadn't wanted to come with him, but by now she ought to have known that with Raoul there was never any soft-pedaling. He was so brutally honest at all times, it could be shocking if she weren't prepared. But she could never be prepared about this.

Where others hesitated, he already knew what he wanted to do and took care of it. Being Raoul, he'd cut through to the heart of the matter because it was his way. No wonder he was the legendary head of the alpine guide club whose name was known far and wide. It was what made him the unique, incredible man everyone looked up to, particularly his close friends and family, who adored and depended on him. Her son, most of all.

He moved closer. "When you got on that plane with Philippe last year, we both knew the strength of our feelings. If you hadn't been in love with me, you wouldn't have gone. It's past time you admitted that your out-of-sight, out-of-mind theory has had the opposite effect. Now that you're back, we need to get married."

"Married—"

His eyes narrowed. "Surely you know me well enough that I would never have suggested we have an affair."

Anger brought heat to her cheeks. She shot to her feet. "Surely you know me well enough I would never dishonor your brother whether it be through an affair or marriage. I loved Eric, and would never hurt him or taint his memory like that."

"No one could ever question your love for my brother, but he's dead. So is Suzanne. It's a fact that neither of them would want to see us go on alone." The words echoed off the walls. "We're alive and in love, Crystal," he said with maddening calm. "There's no dishonor in that. If Eric's and my positions were reversed, he would tell you exactly the same thing."

She knew Raoul was speaking the truth. More than ever she struggled to find the words that would stop this madness before it went any further.

"Aside from all the reasons why we can't be together, can you imagine the pain Philippe would have to suffer with people speculating behind his back whether Eric or you is his father? I can hear it now—

'Is that why Raoul Broussard has been seen about Chamonix with his supposed nephew almost always in tow? When did the coupling occur? How great was the hate between the brothers when Eric was still alive? Is that why they didn't mix their sports? Some rumors have circulated he's not the product of either brother, but the secret son of another man back in Breckenridge. Others say he looks like the Swiss medalist on the ski circuit who had it in for the great Eric Broussard and enjoyed a fling with his Colorado wife for a time.'

"The tabloids would have a field day, Raoul! Scandal would follow him for the rest of his life," she concluded, her voice shaking.

"Scandal be damned, *mon amour.* The lies and rumors will abound forever. It was ever thus. What's more important here? Your fear of what the world thinks, or a happy home with your son who's been begging for the three of us to live together? You said it yourself. Today was a divine day handed to us like a sign. As far as I'm concerned, it was a precursor to the kind of marriage we'll have every day and night for as long as we're both granted breath."

Afraid to listen to any more, she walked closer to the fire, staring at the flames licking upward in the semidark room. He joined her.

"I'm aware of all your fears, Crystal, particularly where our parents are concerned. I know the rest of the list you still haven't mentioned out loud. That's why I'm going to resign from the family business."

Her head reared. *"What?"* she cried in sheer panic.

He studied her features in the firelight. "How else

can we move to Breckenridge if I don't start a climbing club there so I can take care of my new family? In Colorado, it won't be the gossip mill you fear so much here in Chamonix.

"We'll build a brand-new home that will be ours. It'll be a quieter place for us to start out our lives together. Philippe will love it and want to invite his cousins to come and stay. He'll want to bring his school friends home to play. He'll love being near your parents and sisters. We'll make it work so he sees my parents on a regular basis."

His logic made so much sense he had her trembling, but there was a glaring flaw in it. "Don't say anything more. You couldn't leave your family and you know it. They all need and depend on you."

He cocked his head. "Is that how you really see me, Crystal?"

She blinked. "What do you mean?"

"You look at me as a man who holds everyone else up and that's it?"

"No, Rao—"

"Do you imagine I don't need or crave a life of my own?" he interrupted. "That I don't want what every man dreams of? A home and a wife and children who are mine to take care of and raise?"

Crystal bit her lip so hard it drew blood. "Of course I didn't mean that. It's just that your father has been so ill and you've been in business together all your lives."

"But he's getting well, and he has *Maman* and a staff perfectly capable of running Broussard's. He has Vivige and her family. He has their friends. It's time I reached out for what *I* want. A life with you and Philippe. Nothing else will ever do."

His declaration rocked her to the foundations.

"It's what you want, too, so don't you dare deny it," came the fierce warning.

"I'm not—" her voice quivered as she bowed her head "—but what we want isn't possible."

He cupped her chin and lifted it so she would have to look at him. *"Why?"* The question came out more like a hiss.

"For one very good reason. The guilt would eventually destroy us."

His hands gripped her shoulders and shook her gently. "What guilt? Neither of us has ever done anything to be ashamed of. What happened in our hearts was something we had no control over. Do you remember my friend Yves?"

"The one who's wife was killed in a car accident?"

"That's right. They had a baby and her sister took care of it. In time he married the sister. Since then they've had two more babies and are crazy about each other."

She bit her lip. "I didn't realize it was his sister-in-law."

"That's the point. It didn't matter. Two people fell in love in all innocence. It happens, even between the in-laws of siblings. It happened to you and me. As far as I'm concerned, Philippe is our son now."

Crystal shook her head. "You're honestly not worried about what our families would say if they knew how we felt? The pain it would cause them?" she cried in anguish.

His black brows met together. "I can't imagine the fact that we're in love would bring them any pain whatsoever."

Raoul was saying this now, but a day would come—she didn't know when—that he would realize she was right. For all their sakes she had to be the strong one here. "I—I'd like to go back to your parents' house now."

She watched his hands form fists at his sides, visible signs that he was barely controlling himself. "What if I said no," he answered in a grating voice.

"Then you wouldn't be the wonderful man I've been in love with all this time."

When she looked up, the blood had drained from his handsome face. "So this is it?" he whispered in an agonizing tone. "This is your answer?"

Tears filled her eyes. "It *has* to be."

"Nothing *has* to be," he rasped.

"Don't come a step closer—" she cried in despair and backed away from him. "I couldn't stand any more guilt than I already feel since we kissed the other night. I'm not blaming you. I kissed you back, but it was wrong.

"Eric and I got married without telling anyone beforehand, without considering either of our parents' deepest feelings. It was selfish. Cruel. Now to tell them I'm going to marry my husband's brother?" she shrieked. "What kind of a monster would that make me?"

"He passed on a long time ago."

"That doesn't matter, Raoul. I couldn't take being responsible for any more selfish wrongs. Especially one that will impact Philippe when he's old enough to be hurt by gossip and innuendo. I once lived a very selfish life, but no longer. I'm torn apart as it is to even be on the same continent as you."

"Crystal—"

She hardened herself to the plea in his voice. "We're going to get through this holiday like we've done before, and then I'm taking Philippe home with me where we belong. As I told my parents on the phone, if I have to, I'll consult a doctor who will give me something to sedate him so he won't fall apart over leaving you."

Lines bracketed his mouth. Incredulous, he asked, "You would do that to him?"

She nodded her head. "He's *my* son, Raoul. Not yours. I'll do whatever I have to do."

The dark blue eyes she'd loved for so long turned wintry, freezing her insides. She felt him back away from her emotionally as if he viewed her with such distaste, she was repugnant to him. With an instinct born of her love for him, she'd had to be cruel so it would prevent them from making the greatest mistake of their lives.

"Then so will I."

The ominous warning could mean anything coming from Raoul. It terrified her all the way home and throughout the endless night.

It was four in the morning and Raoul still hadn't fallen asleep. His eyes wandered to the hat he'd put on his dresser. When he'd first seen Philippe's hat, he thought it was a signal that Crystal was coming around.

Then he'd seen the American flag and realized his dream of a future with her and Philippe wasn't going to happen. She didn't play fair, either, and might as well have clawed out his heart with that ice pick.

Though he hated to admit it, Philippe was her son and he had no right to interfere. Since she was determined to go back to Colorado and forget he existed, he wouldn't be doing the boy any favors by being constantly available to him until they left.

Not only that, he didn't trust himself to be around her any longer, so there was only one thing to do.

He took another shower and dressed in casual clothes, then he packed a suitcase. Before going out the door he put the hat on his head and left his house for the office. After making a certain phone call, Raoul stayed busy with paperwork until it was time to go over to his parents for Christmas morning festivities.

Christmas morning. What a joke. From now on his life was going to be one of survival, nothing more.

At nine his mother phoned and told him breakfast was ready. He said he'd be there shortly, but told her not to wait for him. She didn't press him. Knowing his mother, she would think what she wanted no matter what excuse he gave her. Raoul had no appetite and felt hollow inside.

Crystal was so entrenched in her unwillingness to see reason, she'd drained the life out of him. When he walked to his car, he felt old....

Once he reached the house, he got all his presents out of the trunk and carried them inside. Everyone was still at breakfast, giving him time to put the packages around the tree. He looked at the fireplace pouring out heat and saw all the shoes lined up, spilling over with candy and little gifts. Two of the shoes were tennis shoes, open with the tongues out and no laces. That was Albert and Philippe's work. His eyes smarted.

"Uncle Raoul—" Philippe came running in the salon toward him with his hat on. He eyed Raoul's hat. "We're twins again."

"We sure are."

The other children followed and soon the whole family had gathered round, agreeing that *Père Noël* had indeed come to this house.

While Raoul hugged the children, he watched Crystal take a seat on one of the upholstered chairs. She avoided his gaze. This morning she was wearing a red sweater with black pants. Her hair gleamed like gold. He would never get over being struck by her natural beauty and finally had to look away before the family noticed him staring.

For the next few hours everyone opened gifts and it was joy galore. Raoul helped Bernard put toys together and set up racetracks. By midafternoon Crystal excused herself and Philippe. Her parents were on the phone. The two of them disappeared from the salon.

While everyone was occupied, it gave Raoul a chance to talk to his father alone for a minute. "The reason I didn't join you for breakfast is because I was on the phone making a flight reservation."

Jules studied him for a minute. "Where are you going?"

"Zaragoza."

"To climb with Des?"

"No. I haven't talked to him. He might not be around or available. I'm planning to stay at the hotel and do some horseback riding."

His father pursed his lips. "I see. When do you plan to leave?"

"There's a late flight tonight, but only if you don't need me. I realize you haven't been out of the hospital long, but you seem so much better and I know Bernard is here for you. All you would have to do is phone me and I'd come home in a shot."

His father patted his shoulder. "You've done everything for me, Raoul. No man ever had a more wonderful son. If you want the time off, take it. This is our quiet time at work and no one deserves it more. I'm feeling fine. Take your break. You need it."

"Thanks. I know Bernard and Vivige will take care of Crystal and Philippe and get them on the plane. She's going home after New Year's Day."

"Ah, I didn't realize."

"She worries about Philippe's attachment to me. Frankly, so do I. That's why I'm leaving. If I'm not around for this next week, it might make it easier when the time comes for their departure."

"That little fellow has been your shadow."

Emotion made his throat swell. "He's like a son to me. I love him." His voice shook.

"He loves you like you're his father."

Raoul fought for a steadying breath. "Will you do a big favor for me?"

"Anything."

"If anyone in the family should ask, even *Maman,* will you tell them I got called away on an emergency? But not a scary one. Think something up that won't alarm Philippe. I don't want him to know my real plans. It'll be easier on him if he thinks I couldn't help leaving. It'll be better this way."

"I couldn't agree more."

He could always count on his father. With that talk out of the way, he joined the boys and Bernard to play with Albert's new racetrack. The women fixed leftovers. Before he knew it, the clock chimed seven times.

While all the children were still involved in their games and Crystal was in the kitchen with Vivige and Arlette, Raoul nodded to his father, who nodded back, then he slipped out of the house, taking his hat with him. Once in the car, he drove out on the main road and headed for Geneva at full speed.

Des didn't know he was coming. It didn't matter. If he had other plans, it didn't matter. All Raoul knew was that he had to get away. At least he was going to a familiar place where he felt at home, and the Pastrana stables were nearby. He would stay there until he knew Crystal had gone.

After doing the dishes, Crystal followed Vivige into the living room. "As much fun as it's been, it's time to go home," her sister-in-law announced. A collective moan filled the salon. "You can play at our house tomorrow."

"Your mother's right," Bernard said in agreement. "Come on. Let's start taking all your stuff out to the car."

It was a scramble to get everything picked up and sorted out. Crystal asked Philippe to help her and they helped carry things so it only took one trip.

"See you tomorrow, Albert."

"See you, Philippe."

"Thanks for everything! Merry Christmas!" Crystal called out and waved them off. "Come on, honey. Let's hurry inside. It's freezing out here. Once we've cleaned up your things, then it's time for bed."

"Uncle Raoul bought me that Match-Up game. He's going to play it with me."

"You can do it tomorrow. Your grandparents are tired. We all want to go to bed."

As soon as they reached the salon, Crystal started gathering their gifts to take upstairs. Philippe put on his hat. "Where's Uncle Raoul?"

"Probably in the kitchen eating."

Her son took off while she carried the first load upstairs. When she went down again, Philippe came running up to her. "Uncle Raoul already went home with his stuff." He looked ready to cry.

Crystal appreciated Raoul slipping out unobtrusively. Even though the news that he'd gone caused her heart to plunge to her feet, she was relieved. It meant avoiding a big production saying good-night to him.

"I told you everyone was tired. He'll come over to Albert's tomorrow. Come on and help me. One more load ought to do it. *Père Noël* brought you so many toys, I don't know how you can figure out which one to play with first."

By the time he'd had his bath and gotten into his pajamas, his eyelids were drooping. They both climbed in bed. She read him a story and halfway through it, he fell asleep. Crystal was afraid she wouldn't be as lucky; but, by some miracle, exhaustion caught up with her. When she awakened the next morning, she was surprised to discover she'd slept all night without dreams.

Philippe was already up and dressed. He was playing with his new Transformer on his bed. "Come on and get up, Mommy. I want to go over to Albert's house."

"First we need to eat breakfast."

"Then hurry."

She showered and dressed in jeans and a hunter green pullover. "Okay, I'm ready."

Philippe grabbed his new Match-Up game and put on his hat. Together they went downstairs to the kitchen. The grandparents weren't up yet. No doubt the poor things were worn out. Crystal fixed them fruit and cereal, then they left for Vivige's.

"I can't wait to play my game with Uncle Raoul."

"You have to let Albert play with you, too."

"I know."

The sky wasn't as overcast as the day before. She thought the sun might actually come out. The warmth would be welcome after the freeze they'd been having.

Once they drove up, the children were thrilled to see Philippe, but he wasn't as enthusiastic when he learned that his favorite uncle in the world wasn't there yet. "Where is he?" he asked Vivige.

"I don't know."

"Will you call him?"

Crystal put a hand on his shoulder. "I'll phone your grandfather. He'll know." She pulled out her cell and made the call.

After Jules's explanation she hung up, having to put on a cheerful face, but inside she felt ill in a way that almost incapacitated her. "Your uncle is at the office doing some work that couldn't be done by anyone else. I'm afraid he won't be able to come over today."

Philippe frowned. "Can we go to his office and see him?"

"No, honey."

"Hey—" Bernard interjected. "Won't I do? I was going to take you kids ice skating."

"Doesn't that sound fun?" She smiled at her son.

Philippe nodded, but the sunshine had gone out of his countenance.

This was the beginning of new pain.

Raoul had backed away from her because he'd gotten the message loud and clear. She shouldn't be devastated by the knowledge that he would never approach her again. Now she understood what he'd really meant the other night when he'd talked about doing what *he* had to do.

"Let's get going before there are too many skaters on the ice," Bernard urged.

Crystal looked at Vivige. "Are you going?"

"No, I'm not good at it."

"Neither am I."

"That settles it," Bernard said. "You two stay here. I'll take the kids and see you in a little while. Fleur wants to try out her new skates."

After they left, she turned to Vivige. "Do you mind if I go get some gas first? I didn't realize until we were on the way over that I was driving on empty."

"Go ahead. My parents called from Lyon. I need to return it. Now would be a good time."

"Okay, see you later."

Crystal got in her car and stopped at the nearest filling station. With that accomplished, she headed for the town center. When she got to Raoul's office, there was no sign of his car anywhere. That sinking feeling in her chest deepened. She hurried back to his parents' house and found Jules in the kitchen eating breakfast.

"Hi." She gave him a kiss. "Where's Arlette?"

"Upstairs on the phone with her sister Delphine. Where's my boy?"

"Ice skating with Bernard and the children."

"Good."

"Except that it isn't."

He eyed her with a puzzled glance. "Why is that?"

"Because his uncle Raoul didn't come over."

"Ah. Sit down and join me."

She did his bidding. "Where is he, Jules? I know he's not at his office. Whatever you know, please tell me because Philippe already suspects something's wrong."

He eyed her for a long time. "Raoul said you're leaving for the States soon. He decided to go away until you were gone in order to make it easier on Philippe. I told him I thought it was a good idea."

She felt the blood drain from her face.

"Crystal—you look like you've seen a ghost. Did he do the wrong thing?"

"No," she whispered in agony. "Philippe loves Raoul too much. I don't know what to do," she confessed with tears in her voice.

"I've seen it coming for a long time," Jules said. "I'm afraid my son loves your son too much, too."

As Crystal nodded, the tears streamed down her face. "They bonded after Eric died."

He shook his head. "They bonded long before that."

Her heart ran away with her. "What do you mean?"

"I loved my second-born son, but he was never the father that Raoul was to Philippe. Nor was he the best husband to you he could have been."

She gasped softly. "I loved Eric with all my heart."

"I know you did, and you stuck by him when most wives wouldn't have. I've never known anyone so loyal. Not one disparaging word from you."

Crystal couldn't believe what she was hearing come out of him.

"But the fact remains that it was Raoul my grandson missed when you took him back to Colorado. And the reality is, Raoul is very much alive and Philippe knows it."

"I know." Her eyes closed tightly. "How am I going to solve this?"

"I know how *I'd* solve it. The solution is so simple, your son has already figured it out."

Her eyes flew open.

"Philippe wants to live with Raoul, but he can't do it without you. He's been asking me why you two don't get married."

What?

"It's true, Crystal," came Arlette's voice. "I heard Philippe say it."

She turned around to discover her mother-in-law had come in the kitchen and had been listening. "It makes perfect sense to your little boy. In his child's way, he knows Raoul's been in love with you for a long time. When Raoul flew to Colorado, I hoped it was love for him that brought you back to us. You *are* in love with him—"

Two pairs of eyes looked at her with such hope and loving affection, she couldn't deny it. "Yes," she said in a wobbly voice.

"I knew it," Arlette murmured.

"We didn't mean to fall in love."

They both smiled at her. Jules reached out to pat her hand. "Of course you didn't. We know you loved our Eric. But he's gone, and now you and Raoul have found love. I think we saw it happening in all innocence before you two did. Don't you realize it doesn't matter what the world thinks? What do they know? Nothing!"

"That's what Raoul said."

"Everyone assumes I became so ill because I was pining for Eric. But the truth is, I was also pining for our Raoul, who barely existed after you left for Colorado. I saw his eyes when your plane took off. The pain and the longing were written there so plainly, a new grief started up in my soul."

"Mine, too," Arlette echoed. "I've never seen a man so completely in love; but he's kept his silence and tread carefully because of your fears."

"Not *that* carefully." She half laughed through the tears. "Last night he asked me to marry him." They gasped in pure joy. "But I told him—I told him… Oh, you know what I told him," she blurted.

"Then only you can fix it!" his mother cried. "I had a talk with your mother on the phone the other day to thank her for the plant. She and your father are praying for the same outcome."

Jules grabbed her hand. "Don't keep Raoul in agony any longer. It would put all of us out of the misery we've been in for the last year."

"You really mean it?"

"Nothing could please our hearts more than to see you two become man and wife and build a new life together."

Arlette slipped her arm around her. "My husband has spoken the truth."

Crystal felt their love, their acceptance, and she started to get excited. In fact she was almost jumping out of her skin for joy. "Where did he go?"

"Spain."

She groaned. "Did he make plans with his friend Des?"

"Not when he left. He told me he was going to stay at the Pastrana Posada in Zaragoza and do some horseback riding."

Crystal had heard him talk of the palace that had been converted into a hotel. She jumped up from the table. "I'm going to fly to Spain with Philippe. Hopefully today. On the way to the airport I'll tell him Raoul had business in Zaragoza and I thought it would be fun if we surprised him."

Jules got up from the table and reached for his phone on the counter. "I'll call the airline and make reservations for you."

"Bernard will drive you to Geneva," Arlette said. "It will be his pleasure. Last night he and Vivige lit a candle at the church for you two."

A boulder blocked Crystal's throat. "Have I told you how much I love the Broussard family?"

"You already know how we feel about you. Run along and pick up Philippe. I'll let you know what time you need to leave for the airport."

Crystal flew out the door and out of the house to her car. She couldn't wait to throw her arms around Raoul and tell him she couldn't live without him.

Raoul's state of mind was so black, he refused to inflict that darkness on Des, so he hadn't let him know he was in Spain. This morning he'd taken out one of the horses and had been gone riding in the fifty-nine-degree temperature. Anything to wear him out so he'd crash when night came.

If his father hadn't been out of the hospital so recently, he would have gone to Puerto d'Ara to do some ice climbing. If he fell or froze to death, it didn't really matter, but he'd promised Jules he'd come right back to Chamonix if he was needed, so he hadn't gone to the mountains.

For once in his life he understood why some people drank their lives away. It was to get rid of the pain that couldn't be forgotten any other way. He didn't want to feel it and would do whatever he had to do to get rid of it.

After letting himself inside his room at the posada, he rang room service and asked for a club sandwich and a bottle of brandy to be brought up. He planned to eat and then drink until nothing registered. Though he rarely imbibed, tonight he needed oblivion.

With that taken care of, he walked into the bathroom to take a long shower. He needed to wash off the sweat after the day he'd put in in the saddle.

CHAPTER NINE

THANKS TO JULES, a limo from the hotel was waiting at the airport in Zaragoza to drive Crystal and Philippe to the Posada Pastrana. After passing through the authentic Moorish gate, the driver came to a stop and unloaded their bag. She'd only packed one.

"Mommy, this looks like the palace in my Aladdin book."

"That's because the people who built the palace where Aladdin lived, also lived in Spain at one time and built this one." If she recalled correctly, Raoul had said it had been erected around 1000 AD. As he put it, this was the Pastrana flagship. It was fabulous. But another time she could appreciate it much more if she weren't shaking with nervous excitement to see Raoul. "Just remember, there's no magic genie."

"Are you sure?"

"Positive."

"Is Uncle Raoul really here?"

"That's what your *grand-père* said."

Philippe's blue eyes looked around in wonder as he took in the Ottoman architecture so foreign to his world. He clutched her hand a little tighter as she walked across a fabulous area rug in the busy lobby to

the front desk. There were three people manning the
counter, two of them male and one a beautiful, black-
haired female. Raoul would have noticed.

"Good evening," she said to the first free person.
"We just flew in and would like the room number for
one of your guests, please. His name is Monsieur Raoul
Broussard."

He gave her a speculative glance. She was wearing
the navy suit she'd worn Christmas Eve. No one came
to a hotel like this unless they were well-dressed. "We
don't give out room numbers, but I can call his room.
What is your name?"

"Madame Broussard."

"You're his wife?"

She would love to lie and tell him yes, but she
couldn't. Even if she were Raoul's wife, the concierge
wouldn't give her a key. A passport proving they had
the same last name didn't guarantee an entree. "No,
I'm his sister-in-law."

His gaze flicked to Philippe. "A moment, *por favor.*"

Philippe held on to her hand while he twisted
around, staring at everything.

The man made the call. After a minute he hung up.
"I'm sorry. There doesn't seem to be any answer."

She checked her watch. It was ten-thirty, past time
for Philippe to be in bed. She was desperate to see
Raoul. Who knew where he might be. She didn't want
to use her imagination. It would hurt too much if she
really thought about all the possibilities after telling
him they could never be together again.

"Would you do me a favor and call your patron,
Senor Desidiero Pastrana? He's Monsieur Broussard's

closest friend. He'll vouch for me so you can give me a key to Monsieur Broussard's room."

The clerk looked shocked, if not a little uncertain. She could hear his mind asking whether she was on the level or not. In case she was and really did know the owner, then he could get in trouble if he refused. She'd put him in a dilemma.

"What is your full name?"

She opened her passport for his perusal. "My son Philippe is with me."

He made a note. "If you'll be seated across the lobby, I'll make an inquiry for you."

"Thank you very much. I appreciate it."

She leaned over. "Come on, honey. The man's going to help us, but we have to wait for a minute." Picking up the bag, they walked over by some plants. There were groups of people talking in Russian and Portuguese.

"They sound funny," he whispered.

"We sound funny to them," she whispered back. He thought about it, then laughed. Philippe's sense of humor was one of his most endearing traits.

Suddenly the clerk left the desk and came hurrying toward her. "Senor Pastrana is on the phone and would like to talk to you."

"Thank you." Inside she was bursting with relief because the clerk had been able to reach Des. Another time she might not have been so lucky. "Come on, Philippe." Once again she clutched the bag and they walked over to the desk. The clerk handed her the receiver.

"Hello, Des?"

"Welcome to Zaragoza, Crystal," came the familiar

vibrant voice. "What a surprise. It's been a long time since we last met in Chamonix."

"Too long. Will you please forgive me for doing something so audacious as calling you like this? Jules told me that Raoul is staying at this hotel. I have to see him tonight. If he's asleep, I need to wake him up. If he's still out somewhere, I'd rather wait for him in his room. This is an emergency or I would never have dared disturb you."

"Is his father asking for him? I know he's been ill." She heard the alarm in his voice.

"No. He's doing very well. This is something between Raoul and I."

After a silence he said, "I see. Put the clerk back on the phone. I'll tell him to give you a card key."

"Bless you, Des. I'll find a way to thank you later."

She handed the receiver back to the clerk, who listened before hanging up, then provided her with a room key.

"Thank you for helping me, senor. What is your name?"

"Jaime."

"Well, Jaime. I'll recommend you to Senor Pastrana."

He broke into a broad smile. "*Gracias, senora.* The room is on the second floor. Take the elevator down the right hall."

Philippe hurried along beside her while she carried the bag. When they got out of the elevator, she turned to the left. Two doors down the hall they came to Raoul's room. Before she unlocked the door, she knocked several times, but there was no answer.

Convinced he wasn't in there, she swiped the card

so the handle would turn and pushed the door open into the dimly lit room.

It was like déjà vu as she came up against a hard body on the other side, but instead of a dress suit, Raoul was wearing nothing but a towel riding low around his hips. His spectacular physique with its dusting of dark hair made her legs go weak. He'd obviously just come from the shower.

"Uncle Raoul!"

Philippe pushed past her and lunged for him, almost dislodging the only article covering him. When she dared look up at his face, she saw a man in a total state of shock. His black hair was still damp. He was gorgeous.

"*Grand-père* said you were here," Philippe informed him. He gazed up at him. "How come you didn't answer your phone?"

Raoul picked him up, but he was still staring at Crystal holding the suitcase as if he were having a hallucination. "I didn't hear it," he muttered like someone in a trance.

"Aren't you glad to see us?"

She didn't think he even heard Philippe. Those midnight-blue eyes were asking questions. "How did you get in here?"

"I asked the clerk at the desk to phone Des. One word from his boss and it was 'open sesame.'"

She thought he might at least smile, but if anything he actually paled.

"Raoul!" she cried in alarm. "Are you all right?"

His jaw hardened. "That all depends on why you're here."

"Are you mad, Uncle Raoul?"

He blinked. "No. Of course I'm not mad." He hugged him.

"Then how come you're not smiling?"

Crystal swallowed hard. "May we come in?"

Raoul stood aside still holding Philippe. After she walked in, he shut the door behind her. She looked around the lavish suite. On the coffee table she saw a covered plate and an open bottle of brandy, but the snifter only held a small amount of it. She knew that if they'd arrived a half hour later, part of that bottle would already be gone.

He'd never been a drinker. Their whole family were temperate in that regard. It gave her an idea of how bad off he was right now.

"Can I go to the bathroom?"

The question seemed to bring Raoul up short. "Of course, *mon gars*. It's through that door over there." Raoul put him down and her son disappeared behind it.

Crystal lowered her bag to the floor. It was probably the first time in their lives Raoul didn't try to help her. His eyes traveled over her as if he were trying to match up his thoughts with what he was seeing.

Before either of them said a word, Philippe came running back out again. "I'm thirsty. Can I have some of your apple juice?"

With that question, Raoul was galvanized into action. "That's not juice. You wouldn't like it."

"Then how come you're drinking it?"

Raoul averted his eyes. "Tell you what. I'll phone down for some apple juice and a grilled cheese. Would you like that?"

"Yes, please. I'm hungry. They only had water and almond nuts on the plane. I don't like them."

"Neither do I. Why don't you get in the bathtub while I order your food. You can squirt my shaving cream in the water."

"Goody!"

While Philippe disappeared, Raoul strode over to the side of the bed and picked up the house phone to place the order. Seconds later she heard the water running and Philippe playing. "This bathroom's *huge!*"

Crystal smiled as she removed her jacket, revealing the sleeveless shell beneath. Curious, she walked over to the coffee table and lifted the cover off the plate. He'd ordered a club sandwich, but he hadn't touched it.

"If you're hungry, go ahead and eat. I lost my appetite," he rasped.

She put the cover back. "I lost mine, too. That's why I'm here."

"What's that supposed to mean?" He was angry and had every right to be since she was the last person he would have expected to see tonight. Crystal couldn't blame him. She'd barged into his room unannounced.

When she looked at him, she discovered he'd thrown on a white bathrobe, the kind issued by the hotel. "I'll be right back."

She put the bag on the chair and opened it. After finding Philippe's pajamas and toothbrush, she carried them into the bathroom. Philippe had been right. It *was* huge, with every accessory known to man. Talk about luxury. Her son was playing around in the enormous tub with the suds.

"This is fun!"

Assured he'd be entertained for a long time with Raoul giving him free rein to his shaving cream, she left the bathroom with her heart in her throat.

He stood there looking powerful, yet remote. "Christmas Eve you said your goodbye to me in indelible ink. Why did you come all this way for whatever it is you want when you could have phoned?" The ice was still in his deep voice.

"Because you don't tell a man you're going to marry him unless it's in person."

When her words reached him, his whole countenance changed. He looked like a man who'd been sent into shock before he started for her.

She ran to him, putting her hands on his upper arms. "You still do want to marry me, don't you? Because I want to be your wife more than anything in this world. I wanted to be married to you before I left for Colorado a year ago, but we know that wasn't possible. Oh, darling, we've wasted so much time. I absolutely refuse to waste any more."

"Crystal—" His cry resounded in the room. He cupped her face, staring into her eyes to read the truth in them.

"Forgive me for putting us through so much pain," she begged him. "This morning when we couldn't find you, I asked your father where you were. When he told me, I broke down. You should have seen me. I was a disaster."

"Tell me about it," he said, his voice shaking.

"Your parents gave us their blessing. I couldn't get here fast enough," she said emotionally. "Raoul, no one's ever made me feel cherished the way you do. I swear to love you the same way so you'll know every second of the day and night what you mean to me. Promise me you'll never let me go."

"As if I could. *Mon coeur*—" But any other cries were muffled because their mouths had taken over to communicate. Free at last to express her love, she couldn't kiss him long enough or deep enough.

"If you hadn't come…" He molded her against him. "It seems like I've loved you forever. To think you were going to leave again— I couldn't take it."

"Neither could I!" She covered his gorgeous face with kisses. "You're my whole world, and have been for a long time."

"Don't ever leave me, Crystal," he insisted. "It would be the end of me."

"I'm in love with you," she cried out. "It's for always and ever. I knew it when you came to Colorado to get me. The sound of your voice went through me like a bolt of lightning. The joy of seeing you in my father's store…" Tears welled in her eyes. "You can't imagine."

"I think I can," he said in a husky voice. "As you can see, I wouldn't leave without you."

"Mommy? Are you crying again?"

She turned around, wiping her eyes. "Philippe! Yes. Yes, I am."

"How come?"

"Because I just told Raoul I would marry him. You see, I've wanted to marry him for a long, long time."

"Goody! How come it took you so long?"

Raoul's hands gripped her shoulders from behind and kissed the nape of her neck, making her feel light-headed. "Because we had a lot of things to work out first, *mon gamin*."

"How soon are you going to get married?" Philippe asked.

"As soon as possible," Raoul declared, wrapping his arms fully around her.

"At the church?"

"Yes."

"With Nana and Grandpa?"

"They wouldn't miss it, honey."

"Are we going to live in your house?"

Raoul kissed Crystal's hair. "I thought we'd build us a new house in Les Mouilles where I have some property. You can plan your own room. If we set it on the ground right, you'll be able to see the peak from your bedroom window. How would you like that?"

Philippe was so happy he put his arms around both of them and squeezed with the strength of ten. The pounding of Raoul's heart steamed into Crystal's. "This is the kind of lovefest I could get used to," he whispered against her ear before biting the lobe gently.

"Hey, somebody's knocking at the door."

"That'll be your food." Raoul released her with another kiss to the neck and moved away to take care of it.

While Philippe ran after him, she grabbed some items out of the suitcase and went into the bathroom. Once she'd removed her suit top and skirt, she slipped on her robe. This couldn't be their first night together, not with Philippe, but she intended to hold Raoul all night just to be sure she hadn't been dreaming all this.

When she emerged, she saw both her men sitting on the love seat eating their food as if they were starving.

Raoul's gaze swerved to hers. She saw the love she felt for him leap from his dark blue eyes back to her.

"Come and join us." He'd ordered juice for all of them and a sandwich for her. The brandy was nowhere in sight.

"Can I tell Albert we're getting married and going to live right by him?"

Crystal nodded. "As soon as we get back to Chamonix."

"Can we go home tomorrow?"

"First thing in the morning." Raoul tousled his hair. "You know what? You need a haircut."

"So do you."

Deep laughter rumbled out of Raoul. The happiest sound in the world.

"Actually, I like your hair this length," Crystal commented, staring at her husband-to-be with unabashed adoration. "I love every single thing about you. In fact I love you so much, it hurts."

"I've been there, remember?" he murmured in a thick tone.

Philippe finished what he could eat and got up. "Where's our bed, Mommy?"

In another heartbeat Raoul got to his feet. "You're going to get your own bed tonight." He walked over to the sofa and turned it into a bed already made up.

"Hey!" Philippe let out a gleeful cry. "How did you do that?"

"Magic," Raoul teased.

"Mommy said there wasn't a magic genie here."

Raoul chuckled in a way that thrilled Crystal to death. "You'd be surprised. Come on and I'll tuck you in."

She went over to kiss her son good-night. He was already half-asleep. Then she got in the king-size bed and waited for Raoul. After he came out of the bathroom, he turned off the lamp and slid under the covers to reach for her. "I can't believe I have you in my arms at last." His strong legs tangled with hers, filling her body with a voluptuous warmth. *"Je t'aime, mon trésor."*

"If you knew the dreams I've had where you whispered those words to me," she confessed, burying her face in his hair.

"I've had the same dreams. Now it's for real. Our lives are just beginning."

"You're six weeks pregnant, Madame Broussard. Everything looks fine. *Felicitations!*" Vivige's OB-GYN smiled down at Crystal. "According to the dates, your baby should arrive November third of this year. You can get dressed now."

Crystal let out a cry of pure joy and sat up on the examining table. This was going to mean everything to Raoul. "I can't wait to tell my husband. We've just built a new house and are moving in over the next two days."

He winked. "Under the circumstances, let him do the heavy lifting." He gave her some samples of prenatal vitamins to start taking.

"I will." *Believe me, I will.*

After Raoul had lost Suzanne and their unborn child, she planned to take perfect care of herself. If she had one concern, it was Philippe, who'd been the light of Raoul's eye. His cute little nose might be put out of joint for a while, but her husband would know how to handle him. Living with Raoul put a whole new name to the institution of marriage. She'd never known such happiness.

The movers would be arriving to pack up everything and take it to the new house. Tomorrow another truck would deliver the things she'd put in storage the year before. Then they'd go shopping for other things they wanted. She knew the first item they would buy!

After she'd taken Philippe to school this morning, she'd gone back to bed with Raoul and they'd made love for the last time in his house. Tonight they'd planned to christen the new house by making love in their brand-new bedroom and create their own memories. Raoul had already confirmed tonight's special date with her before letting her out of bed.

What he didn't know was that when she'd told him she had a few errands to run and would meet him at the new house, she'd gone straight to her doctor's appointment. Raoul had no idea. She'd never had regular periods, so he hadn't realized she was late.

Crystal loved May in Chamonix. Spring had burst into bloom. She was positively euphoric as she pulled up to their new house. *Bien sûr,* it was a chalet, but very modern with large picture windows everywhere and deep window boxes to plant flowers. They loved nature and wanted to bring it into the house as much as possible.

When she got there, no one was around yet. She hurried inside, hardly able to stand it until Raoul got here with the movers and started bringing everything in. The main floor contained a large kitchen and great room, plus a formal dining room and salon.

They'd also included a room and half bath off the

kitchen at the back of the house to hang up coats and parkas and skis and skates and snowboards and backpacks and boots and crampons and ice picks and ropes and anything else.

After walking around, she climbed the staircase to the second floor with its three bedrooms. The third story contained the master bedroom. When they'd designed everything, they'd been satisfied there were plenty of rooms for family and guests. What they hadn't guessed was that there'd be a permanent guest who would come in November.

While she was still going through the rooms, she heard a sound. Raoul was here. Her heart leaped and she hurried over to the landing just as Raoul came bounding up the stairs. In a black T-shirt and jeans or no clothes at all, he would always take her breath away. His dark blue eyes were alive with excitement.

"The truck's here. Our dreams are about to come true." He pressed a deep kiss to her mouth, then raced back down.

Another dream had come true, too, one he didn't know about yet. A secret smile broke out on her face as she followed him down at a much slower pace.

For the next two hours she helped Raoul direct traffic as the movers came and went from the truck. Finally they left. It was a good thing because she was bursting with the news she had to tell her beloved husband.

She grasped his hand. "Come with me. I want to show you something before the family gets here. It's upstairs."

His intimate gaze ran over her body. "If that's your way of telling me you want to christen our new bedroom right now, I'm way ahead of you." Picking her up in his arms, he carried her over to the stairs.

"Darling—after all the lifting you've been doing, you're going to hurt your back."

"Are you telling me I'm an old man already?"

"No." She kissed his jaw. "I just don't want anything to happen to you. I need you more than ever."

He gave her a curious stare. After they reached the next floor, he put her down. Raoul could always read her mind. His powers were in full force right now. "What is it?" For the first time since they'd been married, she heard that old trace of wariness in his voice.

Crystal didn't want him to suffer another second. "We're going to have a baby." While he stood there stock-still, she wound her arms around his neck. "Dr. Simoness confirmed it this morning. November the third's the big day."

With an exultant cry, he lifted her off the floor and swung her around. "Is it true, *mon amour?*" Raoul's eyes glowed like hot blue fires.

"Do you really have to ask?"

He carried her into the nearest bedroom that had a bed and lowered her down, kissing her mouth and throat, and then her stomach. Her husband didn't say anything at first. Instead he let his hands do the talking as they slowly explored her.

She put her hands on top of his. "One of these days you'll feel our son or daughter kicking."

"Crystal—" He moved his hands up and down her arms as a prelude to making love before kissing her long and hard. Eventually he lifted his head. He was trembling. "Do you remember the day I came over to your condo and you were out in front with Philippe?"

Her eyes glazed over. "How could I forget? That was the day I realized I was in love with you."

He nodded his dark head. "It hit us both at the same time. As I stood there with you in my arms, I had a vision of this moment. Once it took hold, it never let go. Now you're my wife and going to have my baby, I can hardly take it in."

"I had the same vision." She drew in another quick breath. "Oh, Raoul..." She hugged him to her and sobbed quietly. "That was such a painful time, but it's over now. You're the great love of my life and you're going to be the most fantastic father."

Raoul rocked her in his arms. "Tonight when we're in bed, I intend to show you how much you mean to me, but right now I can hear voices downstairs."

Crystal could hear Philippe's voice. Vivige had arrived with the children. "When our little boy finds out our news, he's going to need convincing that the world hasn't come to an end because there's going to be an addition to the Broussard family."

He pressed another hungry kiss to her mouth. "Do you know how much I love the sound of those words? Come on. Let's give the family something else to rejoice over."

The left the bedroom and went downstairs as the children were running through the house with delighted cries. Before long Bernard showed up to help, and finally Raoul's parents arrived. Arlette had brought food and some gorgeous flowers to decorate their new abode, as she put it.

With a half-eaten quiche in his hand, Philippe ran over to her. "Mommy? Can we make a special playroom just for Albert and me in the bedroom next to mine?"

"Didn't you know this great room *is* your new playroom?"

"But we don't want other people to play with our stuff. We're going to make a spy shop and we can't let anyone else in."

Her eyes darted to her husband, who was wolfing down his food before tackling his next project with Bernard and Jules, but she knew he was listening intently.

"I'm sorry, honey, but that room is already taken for someone else." She needed to prepare her son, the sooner the better.

Her comment brought the children's heads around. But it was Philippe who blurted, "Who?" Albert didn't look the least happy about it, either. Raoul sent her a secret smile.

"A new little baby's coming to live with us."

"A baby—" Her son looked positively shocked. He put down his food. "How come?"

"They do that sometimes," Raoul announced. He got up from the table and went over to their son. All the adults started to grin.

"I don't want a baby."

Raoul smiled. He hunkered down in front of him. "You'll want this one. It'll be here on November third."

"Papa?" He'd been calling Raoul that since the wedding. "Do we *have* to have a baby live at our house?"

"Absolutely. It's *our* baby. Another Broussard."

Philippe looked at Crystal. *"You're* going to have a baby?"

"Yes, darling."

"Yes!" Raoul cried and let out a whoop that sounded exactly like Philippe when he was ecstatic.

Philippe ran over to his grandparents. "How come Papa's so happy?"

"You will be too when your little brother or sister arrives."

For once their son was speechless.

Raoul eyed Crystal and they both started laughing because they were so much in love and life didn't get better than this.

* * * * *

CLASSIC

Quintessential, modern love stories
that are romance at its finest.

COMING NEXT MONTH
AVAILABLE DECEMBER 6, 2011

#4279 KISSES ON HER CHRISTMAS LIST
Susan Meier

#4280 RUNAWAY BRIDE
Changing Grooms
Barbara Hannay

#4281 FAMILY CHRISTMAS IN RIVERBEND
Shirley Jump

#4282 FLIRTING WITH ITALIAN
Liz Fielding

#4283 NIKKI AND THE LONE WOLF
Banksia Bay
Marion Lennox

#4284 THE SECRETARY'S SECRET
Michelle Douglas

You can find more information on upcoming Harlequin® titles,
free excerpts and more at www.HarlequinInsideRomance.com.

HRCNM1111

REQUEST YOUR FREE BOOKS!
2 FREE NOVELS PLUS 2 FREE GIFTS!

Harlequin® Romance

From the Heart, For the Heart

YES! Please send me 2 FREE Harlequin® Romance novels and my 2 FREE gifts (gifts are worth about $10). After receiving them, if I don't wish to receive any more books, I can return the shipping statement marked "cancel". If I don't cancel, I will receive 6 brand-new novels every month and be billed just $4.09 per book in the U.S. or $4.49 per book in Canada. That's a savings of at least 14% off the cover price! It's quite a bargain! Shipping and handling is just 50¢ per book in the U.S. and 75¢ per book in Canada.* I understand that accepting the 2 free books and gifts places me under no obligation to buy anything. I can always return a shipment and cancel at any time. Even if I never buy another book, the two free books and gifts are mine to keep forever.

116/316 HDN FESE

Name _____ (PLEASE PRINT) _____

Address _____ Apt. # _____

City _____ State/Prov. _____ Zip/Postal Code _____

Signature (if under 18, a parent or guardian must sign)

Mail to the **Reader Service**:
IN U.S.A.: P.O. Box 1867, Buffalo, NY 14240-1867
IN CANADA: P.O. Box 609, Fort Erie, Ontario L2A 5X3

Not valid for current subscribers to Harlequin Romance books.

**Are you a subscriber to Harlequin Romance books
and want to receive the larger-print edition?
Call 1-800-873-8635 or visit www.ReaderService.com.**

* Terms and prices subject to change without notice. Prices do not include applicable taxes. Sales tax applicable in N.Y. Canadian residents will be charged applicable taxes. Offer not valid in Quebec. This offer is limited to one order per household. All orders subject to credit approval. Credit or debit balances in a customer's account(s) may be offset by any other outstanding balance owed by or to the customer. Please allow 4 to 6 weeks for delivery. Offer available while quantities last.

Your Privacy—The Reader Service is committed to protecting your privacy. Our Privacy Policy is available online at www.ReaderService.com or upon request from the Reader Service.

We make a portion of our mailing list available to reputable third parties that offer products we believe may interest you. If you prefer that we not exchange your name with third parties, or if you wish to clarify or modify your communication preferences, please visit us at www.ReaderService.com/consumerschoice or write to us at Reader Service Preference Service, P.O. Box 9062, Buffalo, NY 14269. Include your complete name and address.

HRI1B

Lucy Flemming and Ross Mitchell shared a magical,
sexy Christmas weekend together six years ago.
This Christmas, history may repeat itself when they find
themselves stranded in a major snowstorm…
and alone at last.

Read on for a sneak peek from
IT HAPPENED ONE CHRISTMAS
by Leslie Kelly.

Available December 2011, only from Harlequin® Blaze™.

EYEING THE GRAY, THICK SKY through the expansive wall of windows, Lucy began to pack up her photography gear. The Christmas party was winding down, only a dozen or so people remaining on this floor, which had been transformed from cubicles and meeting rooms to a holiday funland. She smiled at those nearest to her, then, seeing the glances at her silly elf hat, she reached up to tug it off her head.

Before she could do it, however, she heard a voice. A deep, male voice—smooth and sexy, and so not Santa's.

"I appreciate you filling in on such short notice. I've heard you do a terrific job."

Lucy didn't turn around, letting her brain process what she was hearing. Her whole body had stiffened, the hairs on the back of her neck standing up, her skin tightening into tiny goose bumps. Because that voice sounded so familiar. *Impossibly* familiar.

It can't be.

"It sounds like the kids had a great time."

Unable to stop herself, Lucy began to turn around, wondering if her ears—and all her other senses—were deceiving her. After all, six years was a long time, the mind could play tricks. What were the odds that she'd bump into *him*, here? And today of all days. December 23.

Six years exactly. Was that really possible?

One look—and the accompanying frantic thudding of her heart—and she knew her ears and brain were working just fine. Because it was *him*.

"Oh, my God," he whispered, shocked, frozen, staring as thoroughly as she was. "Lucy?"

She nodded slowly, not taking her eyes off him, wondering why the years had made him even more attractive than ever. It didn't seem fair. Not when she'd spent the past six years thinking he must have started losing that thick, golden-brown hair, or added a spare tire to that trim, muscular form.

No.

The man was gorgeous. Truly, without-a-doubt, mouth-wateringly handsome, every bit as hot as he'd been the first time she'd laid eyes on him. She'd been twenty-two, he one year older.

They'd shared an amazing holiday season.

And had never seen one another again.

Until now.

Find out what happens in
IT HAPPENED ONE CHRISTMAS
by Leslie Kelly.
Available December 2011, only from Harlequin® Blaze™

SUSAN MEIER

*Experience the thrill of falling in love
this holiday season with*

Kisses on Her Christmas List

When Shannon Raleigh saw Rory Wallace staring at her
across her family's department store, she knew he would
be trouble…for her heart. Guarded, but unable to fight
her attraction, Shannon is drawn to Rory and his inquisitive
daughter. Now with only seven days to convince this
straitlaced businessman that what they feel for each other
is real, Shannon hopes for a Christmas miracle.

**Will the magic of Christmas be enough
to melt his heart?**

Available December 6, 2011.

Snowflake Bride

JILLIAN HART

Grateful when she is hired as a maid, Ruby Ballard vows to use her wages to save her family's farm. But the boss's son, Lorenzo, is entranced by this quiet beauty. He knows Ruby is the only woman he could marry, yet she refuses his courtship. As the holidays approach, he is determined to win her affections and make her his snowflake bride.

Available November 2011
wherever books are sold.

www.LoveInspiredBooks.com

LIH82891R

ROMANTIC
SUSPENSE

USA TODAY BESTSELLING AUTHOR

MARIE FERRARELLA

Brings you another exciting installment from

CAVANAUGH
JUSTICE

A Cavanaugh Christmas

When Detective Kaitlyn Two Feathers follows a kidnapping
case outside her jurisdiction, she enlists the aid of Detective
Thomas Cavelli. Still reeling from the discovery that his
father was a Cavanaugh, Thomas takes the case, thinking
it will be a nice distraction…until Kaitlyn becomes his
ultimate distraction. As the case heats up and time
is running out, Thomas must prove to Kaitlyn that he is
trustworthy and risk it all for the one thing they both
never thought they'd find—love.

Available November 22 wherever books are sold!

www.Harlequin.com

HRS27753